I0690184

Clydesdale
GOES TO THE HUNT

First Edition

Published by The Nazca Plains Corporation
Las Vegas, Nevada
2009

ISBN: 978-1-935509-35-6

Published by

The Nazca Plains Corporation ®
4640 Paradise Rd, Suite 141
Las Vegas NV 89109-8000

PUBLISHER'S NOTE
Clydesdale Goes to the Hunt is a work of fiction created wholly by *Bob Archman's* imagination. All characters are fictional and any resemblance to any persons living or deceased is purely by accident. No portion of this book reflects any real person or events.

Cover Photos, Christopher Howey and Dragan Trifunovic
Art Director, Blake Stephens

Clydesdale
GOES TO THE HUNT

First Edition

Bob Archman

Part I

Mom said I was cute when I was a baby. I think she was thinking about a six month period somewhere between my first and second birthday. Whenever it was, I sure can't remember anytime anyone thought I was cute.

I was scrawny until I was 12 or 13, then I became scrawny and hairy. I needed to shave daily by the time I was 14. My voice had dropped an octave below Sam Elliot's by then. I was a strapping 5'-4" and 125 pounds. My gym teacher said a quarter of my weight was in hair, another quarter in cock. In case you don't get the drift, that didn't leave much left over for actual body.

I wasn't a dreamboat as a teenager and now that I'm nearing fifty, I'm not any more attractive. I am a nice guy. I have my own security agency in Richmond, Virginia. I had to admit, I felt pretty good about life. My company was doing great, I had lots of friends and I was feeling good about myself. The first 45 years of my life weren't spectacular. My mom was happy with me just making a living. Some of my teachers in school would have been pleased that I just stayed out of jail.

An odd thing happened at Clydesdale & Company. As we grew I became the guy who took the odd or difficult problems. When as I was a cop, my specialty was purse-snatchers and I was known as a "Red-neck" guy who had a knack for apprehending low life. After the big bombing, I moved up in the world. I worked behind the scenes and didn't get any publicity. That was fine with me.

We specialized in handling nasty jobs for other Security agencies. Most of them provide night watchmen, or Mall cops and they aren't well equipped to deal with serious problems. If they had a serial rapist at a Mall parking lot, they'd hire us. We also work for civic organizations and arts groups who have problems in a neighborhood or a purse-snatcher attacking patrons of the Opera or Ballet. We handle those problems quietly, discretely and effectively.

I'm gay and most of my agency is gay. We were the guys rejected by the police because of our sexual likes. Being a good Police Man or Investigator is considered no good if you suck cock, rather than fuck cunt in the real world.

I've never gotten much into the gay scene in Richmond. I've got a job that typically fills up a good 60 to 80 hours a week with strange hours. I can't go to the bars every night, or go dancing until the dawn. I dropped into the Casa Loma Club once for a beer. The Casa Loma is the "in" Gay bar. I was twenty years older than anyone there and suspected I was the only one there who had to shave more than once a week.

I don't mind twinks or femmes, different strokes for different folks I say, but they sure seemed to mind me. No one sat within a ten foot radius of me. I think they were afraid they might catch something. One guy a booth or two away loudly complained that the management was letting old guys in.

I left. Being young is well and good, but you can't stay young. No one can. It seems to me you are setting yourself up for a bumpy ride, if you are counting on remaining young forever. The guys who try have a desperate look I find unattractive. It's difficult to understand gay men who find masculine men ugly. I know there are a lot of them, but it is a puzzling attitude.

Being bald, bearded, and hairy with a deep voice and having a nine-inch cock qualifies me as a man, in spite of my size. I don't find effeminate men attractive, but I don't insult them and I usually don't throw them out of bed when one falls my way. I like bears, but a steady diet of bear meat could get boring. My first introduction to the world of twink gays came unexpectedly one afternoon.

My friend John called me.

"Clydesdale, I've got a business partner who needs some help," John said. John helped set me up in my business and had been a good friend for years. I told him, I was glad to help any friend of his.

"It's not quite that simple," John explained. "This is a business partner who, quite frankly, I don't think of as a friend. I'm not sure I would want him as a friend. He's not my type, socially or politically."

"Is he a jerk?" I asked.

"Not really," John said, "not all the time at least. I just don't agree with anything he stands for. He needs help. His wife was my late wife's cousin. She's a sweet woman, as nice as she can be. Could you come over here and meet with him in an hour or so?"

"He can't come here?" I asked.

"He doesn't want to be seen going into a detective agency," John said. "Hypersensitive." I agreed and an hour later I was in John's living room meeting with Barton Smith, Senator Barton Smith. The Senator was a pillar of the more conservative portion of the Republican Party, resolutely opposed to any progressive measures aimed at improving the quality of life in Virginia.

Barton looked good. He wore an expensive suit, every hair was in place and he had a photogenic jaw, ideal for campaign posters. He was a handsome man, and you immediately sensed he knew it.

Barton didn't shake my hand as I entered. He got two strikes against him with that. "This has to be kept absolutely quiet," he said, "absolute discretion."

"That's my job. That's why people hire us," I said. "What's your problem?"

"I can tell you some of it," he said.

"No, you're going to tell me all of it, or our meeting is over," I said. "There is no way in Hell I'm going to start an investigation knowing "some" of it." He looked at me for a minute, looking pissed.

"I guess you're right," the Senator said. "I'm being blackmailed. It's not exactly for cash. I'm being pressured to send state contracts to the blackmailer. That and give him the names of friends and associates he might be able to serve."

"What kind of serving are we talking about?" I asked.

"Officially he offers stock broker services," Barton said. I knew there was another form of services involved.

"And unofficially?" I asked, having no intention of letting the guy off the hook.

"Sex."

"With whom?"

"The broker."

"The broker is a he?"

"Yes."

"Okay. That clarifies it somewhat," I said. "What's the scam? The hook?"

"The broker is Wilton Manley, he's a young guy. He went to school with my oldest son. Very clean cut, personable, attractive," Barton explained.

"He seemed safe?"

"Yes, he seemed safe," the Senator explained. He sounded disgusted at himself. "He was a member of several athletic and fitness clubs as well as the Country Club and the Jamestowne Club. He met guys in the locker and steam rooms. They got together at his apartment. Several opened up accounts with him to provide an excuse to see him."

"Is this how you met him?"

"No, a friend gave me his name," Barton replied. "He told me, it was safe and very discrete. No need to worry. My friend said, he liked older men and was very accommodating."

"Did he take pictures?" I asked.

"Oh shit, I hadn't thought about that!" the Senator said, as a look of total panic gripped him.

"If he hasn't brought that up yet, I doubt he has them," I said. "So far you are talking about a clever marketing scheme."

"Well he was working for one of the big brokerage houses. Now he's started his own firm, QED Enterprises," Barton said. "I'm on the

Commission for Corporations. I checked up on it. QED Enterprises doesn't exist there. It has no assets and there apparently is no real money in its accounts. It doesn't exist."

"Where are your investments with him?" I asked.

"In Wilton Manley's pocket I assume," Barton responded. "It turned out he left the respectable brokerage house a year earlier than he claimed. Apparently he's been pocketing it all. He must have spent it all and now needs more money. Wilton wants me to give him the names of more potential clients. I told him, I couldn't do that. He told me, I'd be sorry. I have a really bad feeling about this. I'm afraid there's a lot more going on than I know."

"Sounds like a nice guy!"

"I need to find out how bad it is. The political implications are incredible."

"Are all his clients conservative Republicans?" I asked.

"Not all, but most," Barton said.

"A homosexual affair would hurt your career?" I asked. Barton turned white. He was in total panic. I told him, I would try to help him.

"If you know of anyone else involved, have him come by and talk to me. I'd like to get some more leads," I said. Barton said he would try.

I wasn't sure how to proceed. I have to admit my connections to upper class Republicans weren't as good as they might be. I went to see John in his second floor apartment after Barton left. John had connections in the business world.

"Before my wife died I knew them all," he said. "I've lost most of my social connections since then. Once you are no longer regarded as a catch for a widow, interest drops off dramatically. I know where Barton's coming from. He's intelligent, but limited. There are a number of men like him, who never left the farm."

"He didn't look like a farm type to me," I said.

"Today it's the sub division not the farm. In the West End, there are guys who went to Archangel School, went to UVA and then returned to Richmond to work for Daddy's company. Technically, they are well educated and well traveled. They've been to Europe and Vail, but they've never associated with anyone outside of their class. They made friends in kindergarten and have stayed in the same social set," John said. "They are limited and damn proud of it."

John didn't know much about the situation, but he knew someone who did. He called his friend, Magnus. Magnus was made of money and moved in the wealthiest tiers of Richmond's society. Much to my surprise, Magnus wanted to come over. When he arrived I told him the story.

"It all makes sense to me," Magnus said. "Did you know Edward Jannet?"

"No, but the name sounds slightly familiar," I said.

"Did I see his name in the paper a few weeks ago?" John asked.

"Yes. He was a friend of mine. Edward was gay, but deeply closeted," Magnus said. "He had a taste for young men. As you know, that's a taste I don't share. He was very wealthy, slightly effete, prissy and married to Sonia Elverson. Sonia was the heiress to a chemical fortune."

"He killed himself! I remember now," John said. "A month and a half ago, didn't he?"

"Yes, he was a big time contributor to the Republican Party and conservative causes in general," Magnus said. "He was publicly anti-gay, he felt it gave him some protection. I can understand being in the closet, Lord knows I spent enough time in there, but it seemed to me Edward went over the line. Anyway he took an overdose. He left a note saying, he wouldn't betray any more of his friends. No one knew what he was talking about."

"Edward liked young men who he could "help with their careers". They were his personal assistants, or talented boys who needed a break," Magnus continued. "This story you told would explain it."

"There is nothing to connect him to the Senator's story," I said. "It could be a coincidence."

"There is one other thing. A week before he died, he made an appointment for me to meet a new financial advisor. He told me I might like the young man," Magnus said.

"Did you meet?" John asked.

"No. Edward canceled the meeting," Magnus said. "It was a voice mail message. He said his friend wasn't what he thought he was. Edward didn't sound happy."

"How do we get into this?" I asked. "Pretty boys and big time politicos aren't my thing."

"I have an idea, but it may take a call or two to work it out," Magnus answered. He went to the phone.

Magus returned. "If you don't mind, a friend of mine is coming over. Do you know Colin Randalson?"

"The art collector?" John asked.

"That's him. He lives on Monument Avenue in a big Tudor house," Magnus explained. "He was a good friend of Edward's. He may be able to help; Colin was very disturbed by the suicide." The doorbell rang. It was Colin.

Colin Randalson was a distinguished looking man of perhaps 70. He was tall and lanky, with a carefully trimmed beard. He looked like a Victorian Country Gentleman. He also dressed that way. When he opened his mouth, I understood why. He was English. Magnus introduced us.

"Clydesdale, I'm pleased to meet you," he said. "You found the bomber! That was a great piece of work."

"I had lots of help," I said.

"You don't need to be falsely modest. I know the full story," Colin said. "Tell me about this mystery. How does it involve Edward's death?" I explained the scam. Magnus told Colin about his suspicions about the suicide.

"That does make some sense. It could explain it," Colin said. "We were to go to Europe to an auction in London in April. He wasn't thinking about killing himself then."

"Do you know the young man in the case?" I asked.

"I don't, but I know who he is. I go to the Jamestowne Club in the morning. He was never there then, but on the few times I have been there in the late afternoon he was hanging around," Colin said. "He has always been with older men."

"Is there any way for me to get an operative in there?" I asked.

"Not quickly. Most new members of the Club are sons, or grandsons of members," Colin said, adding. "As I recall the application fee is $100,000.00."

"But I have been thinking," Magnus said, "I might go there later this week and see what happens. If your suspicions are correct, I have all the qualifications needed to attract this leech."

"I'm not too sure about that," I said. "Where there is crime, even white collar crime, there is danger. Can we get someone in there as part of the staff?"

"Quite frankly, I'm not too worried about the potential danger. I'm getting on in years. But I can get someone into the club as staff. I'll serve as the bait if you'll provide a fisherman to haul the catch in," Magnus said.

"It's a deal, I said.

"I'm not much attracted to smooth boys, but I can make the sacrifice," Magnus said, sounding like a martyr. I looked at him and realized he was joking.

"What does attract you?" I asked of Colin. "Short, hairy, horse hung detectives maybe?" Colin laughed.

"I don't want to offend, but short and hairy aren't my thing," Colin replied. He paused and slowly said, "Horse hung is a different matter altogether."

"I guess you would like a third of me, then?" I said. Everyone laughed.

"If it's a third of you, I'd really like it!" Colin said. The doorbell rang. It was Larry, the artist who lived next door. John introduced him to Colin. Larry knew Magnus and me well.

"I had just got my hot tub working again after the engine burned out last month," Larry said. "I was going to ask you over for a re-christening, but since you have company, I'll give a rain check."

"Don't miss out on the fun on my account," Colin said. "I'm leaving anyway."

"You're free to join us, if you'd like," Larry replied. "It's big enough for all of us."

"No swimming trunks," Colin muttered. "I'd better be going."

"No one's ever worn trunks into my tub yet. We're a friendly group of guys here. I guess you could say the dress code is informal," Colin perked up. He was interested.

"Let's go then!" Magnus exclaimed. We all trooped next door and over to the tub. It was a six-man tub sitting in a stained glass green house added to the rear of Larry's house. It was bright and sun lit, but you couldn't be seen from the outside. I stripped and got into the tub.

"This place is incredible," Colin observed as he slowly undressed. "Who did the beautiful paintings in the living room? They're stunning."

"I did," Larry said. "I've been making a living renovating houses, so I've been keeping my paintings to myself for the last ten or twelve years." Larry was handsome, muscular and had beautifully formed genitals. He had a perfect cock and balls. The paintings weren't the only things in the house Colin admired.

We talked and Colin turned out to be a nice guy. He was interested in everything, funny and entertaining. I was getting hot, so I sat on the edge of the tub to cool off.

"Damn, when you said you were horse hung, you weren't kidding!" Colin cried. "It doesn't look real."

"It's real enough, Colin," Magnus said. "And if exercise can make a cock bigger, Clydesdale has done his bit to maintain it!"

"When I first saw him I would have said "Pony" rather than Clydesdale, I think. Now I understand the nickname," Colin added. "I've never seen such an impressive tool on such an ugly man."

"I like you too," I said.

11

"Oh, I'm sorry!" Colin said, genuinely shocked. "I didn't know what I said, believe me, I'm never that rude! It's just the contrast. There is so much cock and so little of you!" I laughed. We all had a nice conversation. Magnus had to leave.

When Colin left it had started to rain. He had walked over, so I offered to drive him home.

"I hope you don't think I am a complete fool after what I said to you," he apologized again. "I have heard nothing but the most glowing reports about you from my friends."

"Forget it," I said. "To tell you the truth, a lot of guys change their opinions about me when they see my cock. If I could leave it hanging out, I'd be a real popular guy!"

"That you would," Colin said. "You aren't a physical type that attracts me, but I am a size queen."

"You are torn between opposite desires. I know the feeling," I observed. "I'm not attracted to smooth men, but I do make the sacrifice, sometimes."

"I know the feeling," Colin admitted. "Are you a top?"

"I sure am," I said as I looked at Colin. I could tell that was what he wanted to hear. Five minutes later we were in his bedroom and I was lubricating my cock. My head was at his hole and I was applying some pressure.

His ass was more like a mouth with lips that caressed my cock head. There was absolutely no resistance. I took it slow to enjoy the ride. Colin could do more with his ass than some guys could do with their mouth. There was no resistance, but his tunnel lining was bonded to my cock. Colin's ass was a full-fledged sex organ and I was the organ grinder.

"Are you in all the way?" he asked.

"You got another three or four inches," I said. "Do you want me to stop?"

"Shit no!" was the decisive answer. I shoved the last few inches in Colin's quivering ass, he almost fainted in pleasure.

Part 2

Colin told me later, my cock hit some spots in his ass that had never been touched before. Colin lost all of his English reserve once my cock got deep. He moaned, he cried, he whimpered and shivered in response to any and every movement I made. I enjoyed it too.

It really does your ego good to fuck a guy who is that enthusiastic. I was feeling as if I was the world's greatest lover. His love tunnel quivered, shook and twitched as I pumped him. He also liked it hard and deep. He liked it when I made only small movements; rubbing my cock head on the same spot in his ass, over and over again.

He was in good shape for his age, well tanned and I had the impression he had shaved his chest hair to keep it even. He had an average cock and good low hangers. Once we got going his cock grew a size. I lubricated it and stroked Colin's meat as I rammed his ass. He begged me to not stoke his cock. It was too sensitive.

I didn't think he was sincere about that, so I kept on doing it. I was stroking his cock, pinching a tit and fucking him at the same time. I figured I'd get all of his erogenous zones operating in unison. I'm not a control freak, but it is nice to have complete control of a guy's sexual apparatus some times.

Colin was an open book once he was fully aroused, so I knew when he was getting close to shooting. I would slow down and let him cool off some. As soon as he calmed down enough, I'd rev him up again.

I was better at judging him than myself. I was feeling good when I realized I was way beyond the point of no return. I pulled out and sprayed a pint or two of cum all over his tanned body. I guessed right about that too. Colin shot off, using my cum to lubricate his cock. We showered and I went home.

Colin and Magnus had all the makings of good detectives. Colin found out Wilton Manley's base of operation had moved from Richmond to the Culpepper Hunt Club in the Piedmont area. The Culpepper Hunt Club was exclusive beyond any reasonable level, all male, all white, all Protestant and all Republican. It catered to a national crowd of lobbyists and politicos and multi-millionaires. Most members used it as a home-away-from-home when they were pulling strings in Washington.

That's not exactly right. Some were pulling strings. Some were having their strings pulled. Colin had connections there and said he could get an operative into the place if I needed one.

"It would need to be a locker room attendant to do any good," I said.

"That's not a problem," Colin replied. "The manager was a former employee of mine. I got him the job and he owes me. My reference neglected to point out several rough spots in the man's resume, if you get my drift. Quite frankly, I can get anyone, anywhere you want."

I had already placed Lonnie in the Jamestowne Club locker room. I knew Magnus and Colin were sensible men, but they were also take-charge types. I didn't want them unprotected. Lonnie had a checkered past, but had done favors for half of the waiters in Richmond at one time or another. He had slept with the other half. He was a compulsive gossip and as such was never regarded with suspicion when he asked questions.

I decided to check out the Culpepper Club myself. I wasn't particularly well known in Richmond and no one knew me outside of town. I buzz cut my head and trimmed my beard into a goatee. I added glasses and I don't think my Mom would have recognized me.

Freddy, my business partner was checking up on the financial aspects of the case. He was a white- collar crime specialist and he got his collection of retired policemen computer nerds to check up on QED Enterprises. I drove off to the Culpepper Hunt Club deep in rural Virginia

The Club was on the lower slopes of the Blue Ridge. The Club's road was unmarked, except for a small sign adorned with letters "CHC". A half-mile up the road, I could see the clubhouse. It overlooked a perfectly manicured golf course which wrapped around a large man-made pond. Here and there I could see small guest cottages peeking out from the woods on the edges of the fairways.

As far as I could tell the Hunt in Hunt Club was a polite fiction. I did find they had stables tucked in the woods and riding trails, but most of the members were hunting for birdies and par rather than foxes. They did have an actual hunt twice a year, but that was in the fall, and not during my tenure there.

I went in to the Manager's Office. The Manager, Thomas Wilson, was a slick, manicured 45- year-old man. He was perfectly dressed as a country gentleman. His clothes were informal, but very expensive. The walls of his office were embellished with English Sporting prints. From my conversation with Collin I knew the only riding he did was on the rock hard cock of a man who could help him with his career.

"You're a friend of Colin's?" he asked. I nodded. He looked surprised. "You're not his type." I smiled.

"You can't see the part of me that is his type," I said. Thomas laughed.

"I forgot about that," he said, still laughing. "I remember now. I never play with the staff, but if you decide to leave, come by and see me. It will sure help your severance pay!" He winked at me. "You will work as an attendant in the health club in the evening, from 2:00 until closing at 10:00. The Club Manager will tell you what you need to do." He began to whisper. "The manager is a real prick, not open minded at all. Be careful around him. The guests are officially close-minded too, but most are here away from their wives and mistresses. I guess you can fill in the rest."

"You don't mind if the staff entertains the members?"

"As long as the guest takes the lead, don't worry. Never take the first step," Thomas continued. "The tips are really good, I've been told." He took me to the Athletic Club and introduced me to Bernie, the exercise room Manager. Bernie was a retired Army Drill Sergeant. It took me thirty to forty seconds to realize he was gay as a goose and terrified someone would find out. He was masculine and macho, but I knew he was gay. Half of the guys in Clydesdale & Company had been like that at one time.

Bernie gave me a tour and told me what to do. I knew what he wanted and asked the right questions. I asked if he had a checklist of things that had to be done to close up the place. That was exactly the sort of thing Bernie liked. He had a checklist and it was detailed to the degree I expected. I also asked how to reset the temperatures in the Steam room and Sauna. I assumed the club had the usual number of men who had to have the temperatures at a dangerous level in order to prove their manhood. I guessed right.

I had a bedroom next to the locker area, so I would also be on call, if anyone wanted a late night exercise session. The bedroom was no frills and I was expected to use the main shower room for my own personal use. I said that didn't bother me. The first night on the job was uneventful in the beginning. Nobody knew who I was, so everyone was being careful. I handed out towels and made small talk with the guests. The regular Exercise Instructors were off at 6:00, so I was the only staff member there in the evening.

Wilton arrived at 6:30 with two other young men. I had seen his photograph, so I knew what he looked like. He was better looking in the flesh than his photo indicated. He was blond, tanned and healthy. The boys with him looked much younger than him. I knew they were in their mid-twenties, but one could have passed for 16 if you didn't look too closely.

The trio disbursed and soon each was exercising next to an older man. They were talking and from what snatches of conversation I could hear they knew the older men. Several of the younger men glanced at me from the corner of their eyes.

They vanished into the showers and steam room afterwards. I was supposed to check out these areas every fifteen minutes, but I altered the pattern. I asked them if they would let me know if anything needed to be done as they left. I told them, I didn't like to walk in on guys unannounced. I made points with the guests that way.

I made an exception for one older man. He was way overweight and had been exercising vigorously with the youngest looking boy, Jason. I had a feeling he was overdoing it. They went into the steam room. The boy left after five or six minutes. He said it was too hot. Five minutes later I realized the man was still in there. I went in.

He had fallen asleep. When I tried to rouse him, he didn't react. I turned off the heat, propped the door open and got him out. I found a Medic Alert bracelet and realized the man was diabetic. Oh, shit! I thought as I yelled at one of the guests to call the Club Doctor. I was able to revive him and get some orange juice into the man before the doctor arrived. The man was okay. After this, I was a hero.

I had been afraid there would be a long, getting acquainted period before the men would accept me and forget I was there. Once the story got out, I went from being the new man to a trusted retainer in a day. My mom had told me that eventually servants disappear. She was a Nurse and told me after being with a patient for a while you become part of the wallpaper. She was right.

By the time we got the man out of the locker room, it was time for me to close up. I was covered in sweat and the man had spit up on me so I smelled.

"You need a shower," one of the guests said. He had been helping with the fat man and was the only guest left in the area.

"I sure do. I'll do it after I close up. The steam room and this area need to be washed down anyway. That will take a while."

"I'd be glad to help," he said. "After what you did, you deserve some help."

"Don't worry. I can take care of it," I said, as I got the hose out of a storage closet. He went off to the shower room and I heard him turn on the water. I took off my tee shirt and wet pants and hosed down the rooms wearing my boxers. After I was done, I put the hose back

The man looked in. My boxers were soaked and my cock was clearly outlined in the thin fabric.

"Why don't you join me in the shower?" he asked.

"The staff isn't allowed to shower in the main locker area when guests are present."

"Think of yourself as my guest," he said. "Come on in and clean up." He caught a glimpse of my cock and I was sure he wasn't that interested in my hygiene. I took a good look at him for the first time. He was well over six feet and was thirty or forty pounds overweight. He had a football player's build. He was balding, with an even coat of curly, brown hair on his chest.

"I guess there will no problem with that," I said. We went into the showers and I took my shorts off.

"The names Charley," he said, shaking my hand.

"Wildridge here," I said, afraid my nickname as Clydesdale might give me away. I turned the water on. The man wanted to get a good look at my cock, but was too uneasy to stare. I washed my hair and rinsed it with my eyes closed to give him an uninterrupted viewing time. When I opened my eyes I noticed he was at half-staff.

"Sorry about that," he said.

"Nature takes its course whether you want it to or not," I said. "I've got no problems with it. You've got a nice one there."

"Yours is incredible," Charley said. "It's a beauty."

"We all get to play with the hand we're dealt. There's nothing wrong with a cock any way it's served, soft, hard or medium rare, as far as I'm concerned." He was getting harder.

"I'm really embarrassed," Charley said.

"No one's looking except me and I like the view," I said. I was washing my cock now and peeled the skin back exposing my cock head. I rinsed it off and pulled the skin over it again. Charley looked disappointed. The poor guy wanted to get something on, but was too timid. I turned off the water and dried off.

"Would you like to drop by my room for a drink," Charley asked.

"I'd love too, but it's late for me and I'd better get some sleep," I replied. The poor guy looked crestfallen. My clothes were all soaked; I collected them and went toward the door.

"Are you going to your room naked?" he asked.

"Nope, let me show you a secret," I said as I went into a storage room. "Follow me."

I flipped off the lights in the locker room and went to the back of the storage area. There was another door there. I unlocked the door and was in my bedroom.

"Here we are. I have no idea why the room is connected to the lockers, but it is," I said. I stroked my cock a few times. Charley looked as if he had died and gone to heaven.

"Let me help you with that," he said as he reached over and fondled my meat. I stroked his cock as he stroked mine. "Be careful, I'm really close."

"What can I do to slow you up some and have a nice time?" I asked. Charley looked at my cock and licked his lips. "Go ahead and do it. I don't mind." He looked at me, uncertainly. I smiled. "Believe me, I got no problem! Go for it." He dropped to his knees and stared at my cock.

"It tastes better than it looks," I said.

Charley was inexperienced, but willing enough. It was clear he was new to cock sucking. It always surprises me when I encounter a middle-aged man who is new to the scene. He stuck his tongue out and licked the puckered skin enshrouding my cock head. He built up some nerve and took the entire cock head into his mouth.

I felt his tongue slowly licking the pucker and working his way to the head. When he found my piss slit, he flicked his tongue back and forth several times.

He looked up and asked, "Am I doing it all right?"

"You sure are. Just take your time," I said. I reached down and felt his cock; he was dribbling precum. I took some on my finger. "Do you ever taste your own precum?" I asked. He nodded yes. I pulled back my foreskin, rubbed his precum on my cock head and slicked the skin back.

He began sucking me with gusto. A minute later he looked up again. "Is that your precum I taste now? It's sweet."

"It sure is, Charley. I think of it as my own special sauce. Are you okay with it?" He smiled and went back to sucking me. We took a few breaks and I sucked him some. After a half hour, Charley graduated from the Rookie stage of cock sucking to the confirmed cock hound stage.

It was hard to suck him because he was so close to shooting. He had a long, comparatively thin shaft with a big mushroom. Oddly, the shaft was hard as steel, but the head remained soft and tender. I guessed a hard shaft with a cushion on the tip might be good in an ass.

"I'm going to shoot if you keep on doing that," Charley whispered. I didn't stop. Charley's whole body shook as he ejaculated. He had nice balls, but he must have been saving for weeks. When he stopped I had a mouthful of man seed.

"What can I do to get you off?" he asked. I spit the sperm out, on my hand and coated my cock with his man seed. I had been planning to jack off using it as lubricant. I stroked five or six times.

"I'm shooting now!" I cried. I figured he'd like to watch. He started licking his cum off my cock and didn't stop when my seed mixed in it. We both cooled off after our climaxes.

"Damn Charley, you're good!" I cried. "That was hot."

"Did I do it right?" he asked. Charley was a big and impressive man. Somehow I got the impression he was not self confident sexually. "I've never done that before."

"It couldn't have been any better. Are you okay? Sometimes new experiences can be a shock."

"It blows my mind," Charley said. "Is sex with men always this good?"

"With me it is," I said. "Or at least, I try to make it that good. Why do it if you don't have a good time?"

"Those boys have been coming on to me and I had no interest all," Charley explained. "I guess they are cute, but I can't visualize sex with guys younger than my sons. You turned me on."

"I don't want to kill the romance, Charley, but I'm afraid it was my cock you liked. There is something about a big cock that excites most guys, straight or gay."

"Well, whatever it was, it did a job on me," Charley replied. "I'd better be getting back to my room."

"Charley, feel free to drop in again," I said. "This has been nice."

I wasn't too sure he would be back. Some guys get worried and think they have gone too far. Gay sex is easy for the flaming queen types, but is also easy enough for self confident, sexually driven men. It seems it's the uneasy middle ground of weak or unsure men who have a problem. I didn't know where Charley fit.

The next morning, Bernie cross-examined me in detail about the incident in the steam room. He was satisfied I had done the right thing. I asked him if there were other men in poor condition over exercising. Bernie laughed.

"We usually have the opposite problem. No exercise at all. Zippo, Zilch!" he said. "This isn't a high powered athletic club. Most want to do just enough to be able to tell their wives they exercised while they were away."

"There were some younger guys here last night," I said. "Are they better about exercise?"

"I don't really know. There's something strange about them. They seem to talk to the older guys a lot. Never give me the time of day," Bernie replied. "There are a lot of snooty guys here, but none are quite as rude as those pretty boys. I don't know how they get in here. They aren't related to anyone as far as I can tell."

"They seemed to hang around the older men," I said.

"I've noticed that too," Bernie said.

"You're a good looking man. If they were interested in the obvious, they'd be after you," I said.

"I'd never thought of it like that," he replied. "I must be too old for them. You didn't scare them away? You don't look like their type at all."

"Somehow I got the impression I would need to have a bigger bank account to be attractive to them. I would bet they have standards. As far as I could tell they didn't notice I was here. They were too busy to notice the staff. They had bigger fish to fry."

Bernie glanced at my crotch. He smiled. "I kind of doubt that." Bernie had loosened up a bit since the day before. He didn't make a move, but he had noticed.

I asked him if there was a first aid kit in the exercise area. I wanted to get the conversation back to business. Bernie was my type and I wanted to take my time.

Bernie looked shocked. "No, but I need one. I'll take care of that. Are you trained in first aid?"

"My mom is a nurse. My Dad died when I was a kid and Mom and I talked a lot. She's a smart woman and knew what to do in an emergency. I was a curious kid and I picked up a lot."

Part 3

I made big points with Bernie for cleaning up the shower and steam area. Near death experiences were no excuse in his mind for being sloppy. After that I gave the same report to Thomas, the club manager.

I was off duty until 2:00 so I went to my room and made some cell phone calls to my office. Lonnie was well ensconced at the Jamestowne Club and was making a move on one of the gigolos. Lonnie moved in odd circles and knew a party boy when he saw one. Lonnie was conventionally handsome and had guessed the kid wanted some younger cock. Fortunately, the young man wasn't perceptive and liked to talk a lot. Lonnie thought he'd have some real information shortly.

Frank, my business partner, told me the financial information of QED was exceeding complex and confusing, but he had strong suspicions. "It smells as if there's a week old fish, stinking in the sun somewhere. It's right under my nose, but I can't find it," Frank said. "By the way, Magnus wants to talk to you. Will you be there for a while?" I said yes. Fifteen minutes later Magnus called.

"Clydesdale, Colin and I have been having a great old time," Magnus said. "I'd never thought I'd get to play Mata Hari at my age, but I have this one boy drooling for my cash and doing everything but washing the windows and cleaning the gutters to get my account! It's great fun."

"What's the scam?" I asked, "The M.O.?"

"The boy, whose name is Temple, cozies up to me and chit chats. He says I remind him of his dear departed Grand Dad. Temple exercises shirtless, is smooth and hung, incidentally," Magnus explained. "Polyester shorts with no jock. It's discrete, but leaving nothing up to the imagination. Somehow he ended up in the shower with me and then the steam room. He went straight for my cock as soon as he got the chance."

"It's hard work, but someone has to do it," I remarked. Magnus laughed.

"You got it!" Magus answered. "The next night he was there at the same time I was and this time he mentioned he was a financial advisor. Temple said he had some new, tax-free investment opportunities for persons in certain tax brackets. He was quite a good actor and it seemed very off the cuff and informal. I told him I was fully invested."

"He let it drop, but when we were in the steam room, I mentioned I had a small apartment near the club. We might go by where we could talk in private. The boy was more than willing. Fifteen minutes later, we were having a drink and talking about his investment opportunity. A half hour after that, he was in bed and I was fucking him to kingdom come," Magnus said. "I haven't fucked anyone that hard or long in years." Magnus was a good top, and he was enthusiastic about Temple's ass if not the man himself.

"Did he like it?"

"Eventually," Magnus said. "He wasn't anywhere near as experienced as he thought he was and there was a steep learning curve. I had taken a Viagra. For the first hour Temple was tight and fighting me. I needed to do some sphincter dilation exercises. After then he was mine. He was a quivering sex toy. His ass was wide open and every time I re-entered him I hit the jackpot. There was no part of his sexual apparatus that wasn't raw and sensitive. Everything my cock head touched in his ass left him twitching in pleasure."

"I sent him home and I will bet he won't sit down for a week," Magnus continued. "I said, I'd think about the investment, so the poor boy has to come back for the sale. I asked, for a written prospectus too. Temple wasn't too happy about that."

"When is your next meeting?" I asked.

"I will be going back to the club on Friday. We'll see what happens then."

"Be careful," I said.

"I'll do that," Magnus answered. "But I see that you already have an operative at the club. Is he watching?"

"Was he that obvious?" I asked.

"Not at all, but I recognized him," Magnus hung up. I spent the rest of the morning wandering around the place getting the lay of the land.

Work was the same as the day before except without the dramatics. The word was out about my rescue and several men thanked me for the quick thinking. After dinner several men arrived to exercise. This is when I encountered several high-ranking members of Virginia's power establishment. This wasn't particularly pleasant. I met Governor Tyler Johnson. He had been one of the leaders of the Massive Resistance campaign in the 1960 that had closed many of the public schools in order to keep black people out.

I don't follow politics much, but he always struck me as a mean bastard. Officially, he had reformed and was now an "elder statesman". I didn't believe it. Johnson didn't ask for things, he demanded them. He was rude, abrupt and looked at the staff as if we were dirt.

Wilton was there and he sent one of his boys to the elderly man. This was the same one who had left the guy in the steam room the day before. The night before I had learned the kid's name was Jason. Jason was rude too, so I assumed the two deserved each other.

I moved around the exercise area, cleaning and straightening up, so I was able to catch small snippets of the conversation. I played the perfect servant, "Would you like another towel, Sir?" or fetching them drinks. As I passed Johnson and Jason, I heard Jason saying, "You're a legend, I'm so honored to meet you. You were our last sensible Governor. No one since you has stood up for the rights of White men." Johnson was eating it up.

Jason was 25-26 but looked a few years younger. He was blond, with a killer smile and pure white skin. He was healthy looking, but obviously never went outside. He was wearing polyester shorts and his cock was both big and evident. The next time I walked by, Jason was saying, "It's a great investment opportunity, just right for a man at your level of achievement." From Magnus' conversation of this morning, I could fill in the rest. Oddly, the former Governor was calling the boy "Jimmy". I had thought his name was Jason.

As I was closing up, Johnson was standing in the showers, alone. He wasn't showering. He was just standing.

"Can I help you sir?" I asked. Johnson stared.

"Where is my bedroom?" he asked.

"In one of the guest cottages," I answered. "You need to go to your locker and get dressed." Johnson didn't react. "Where is your key?" I asked. "I can help you find your locker."

"I don't know where it is," Johnson replied. He had a towel wrapped around his waist and the key was pinned to it. "The funniest thing happened to me," the old man said, "I had somehow gotten the idea Jimmy was dead, but he's fine. Just fine." Johnson wasn't the same man I had met earlier, he was smiling and quiet.

I took him to his locker and got him dressed. I found his cottage key and took him there. After ringing the bell, a distinguished looking black man answered the door.

"Is this Governor Johnson's cottage?" I asked.

"Yes it is," the man answered. "Come in Governor, it's time for bed." The Governor looked lost. "I'm Raleigh, the Governor's chauffeur and valet. Please come in."

"He seems to be a bit disoriented," I said.

"Tell me what happened," Raleigh asked. I told him.

"He's been getting forgetful lately," Raleigh said.

"This is a lot more than forgetful," I said.

"I'm afraid so," the man said. "I've been worried about it. He's been living in the past, talking about Jimmy as if he just stepped out."

"Who's Jimmy?"

"His son, Jimmy, committed suicide thirty years ago," Raleigh said.

"Who in hell let that man in this house?" Johnson screamed. He was enraged. "I told you not to have any of your low life friends into the house! What Sarah saw in you, I will never know!" Johnson's personality had changed again, back to the dark side.

"Governor, he walked you home from the club. It's dark; you know we can't have you falling again, like the last time you were here!" Raleigh said. "I have your drink ready in the bedroom."

"Did you make it nice and strong, the way I like it?" Johnson said. "You're always trying to short change me, drinking it yourself! Like all your kind." I'd have decked the guy, but Raleigh just smiled and directed the governor to his bedroom.

"Wait for me a few minutes, if you would," Raleigh whispered as he left the room. This gave me a chance to look around. There were a few old photographs in gold frames. One was obviously an old campaign portrait of the Governor looking determined. Another was of a beautiful woman with three children, two girls and a boy. The boy was blond and perhaps 14. I thought of Jason, and didn't like what I was thinking.

"He's settled, I have peace for eight hours at least," Raleigh said "I appreciate you bringing him home, I was afraid he'd get lost. I'd really appreciate it if you wouldn't mention this to anyone. I've got to get his daughters to do something about it."

"I don't talk about people I don't know," I said. "How do you stand living with that asshole?" Raleigh laughed.

"It ain't easy. My mom was Miss Sarah's maid. Miss Sarah was the Governor's wife, as sweet and kind as a single woman could be," Raleigh explained. "When mom got sick, Miss Sarah took care of her, paid for everything. Even when Mom couldn't really work anymore, they'd pretend. Mom was too proud for charity, so she would go to Miss Sarah's and Miss Sarah would pretend Mom was still taking care of her. It was actually the other way around. I started working around the house and just stayed. Before Miss Sarah died she asked me to take care of the Governor. I said I would."

"Is he always a jerk?"

"As far as I can tell. He's actually been pleasant once or twice in the last few months," Raleigh said. "I'm afraid it may be part of the disease."

"Alzheimer's?"

"That's the way it looks to me," Raleigh said. "I'll stay with him to the end. It's lucky I'm not the marrying kind. It's turning into a 24 hour a day job."

"I'm not the marrying kind either," I said. Raleigh looked at me and smiled. "But, I'm not sure I could put up with the abuse you get from that ass hole." I adjusted my cock in my pants. Raleigh rubbed his crotch.

"Are you new here? I haven't seen you before," Raleigh asked.

"New, as of yesterday. Will's the name. I need to get back to my room," I said. "Why don't you drop by and we can have a beer?"

"I might just do that, but my room's a lot closer," Raleigh said. He looked at me for a few seconds. "I was kind of thinking you are a horny guy who wouldn't mind some release."

"Raleigh, you're a perceptive guy," I said. "And I don't mind helping a friend out either."

"Do you have any problem with size?" Raleigh asked. "I'm a big guy."

"No problem at all," I said. "I've been told I'm good for a white guy." We went back to his room. Raleigh was about 50 years old, 5-10, solidly built, with a prematurely white, bushy beard. Naked he was muscular with a hairy chest. His body hair was white near his shoulder and graded to pitch black at his thick pubic bush. His cock was a beauty, thick and long with a big head. He had bull balls too.

"Damn it, you are good for a white man!" he observed when he saw me naked. "I'm not sure I've ever seen so much white meat in the flesh before."

"Thanks," I said. "You've got a cock that must give chills to the good ol' boys the Governor associates with."

"That it does," Raleigh said laughing. "Let me tell you one strange thing. Blacks may scare them, but black cocks turn them on. You'd be amazed how many I've fucked. Some get real excited."

"Forbidden fruit tastes better?" I suggested.

"That may be it. Old wives tales about black guys' sexual prowess may be part of it too. They may not want their daughters to try it out, but there's a lot of curiosity," Raleigh said. "If you're a closeted, red neck, size queen, my cock is a dream come true." He got on his knees and began licking my cock. I was still soft and he took my cock in his mouth. He worked his tongue inside the foreskin and licked my cock head. As my dick began to swell he continued to suck and he got distinctly more enthusiastic as my cock reached full size.

He was trying to deep throat my entire cock while forcing his tongue down my piss slit. Raleigh was a real cocksucker. My cock was in the throat of a master. We relocated on the bed and moved to the 69 position. You can fake being excited, but you can't fake precum. Raleigh's cock was drooling the sweet goo. It was a steady flow interrupted by big spurts, when he got particularly excited.

"Damn, you're good!" I said when we took a breather. "Is there any chance you are a bit of a size queen yourself?" Raleigh laughed.

"You found out my secret," he replied. "I hate to say it, but I seem to be turned on by big red neck meat."

"If you don't slow up some, you are going to be the proud recipient of a load of genuine, high test, redneck, baby making juice," I said. "You're good."

"Is there any chance you would like to shoot that load in my ass?" he asked. "Are you into that?"

"Boy do you know the way to my heart," I answered. We readjusted our positions. He had some lube beside his bed and I coated my cock. Raleigh got on his back on my bed. I got his legs on my shoulder. This opened up his ass, so I lubricated it, working several fingers into his hole. He loved it. I hoped he would like my cock as much.

I had nothing to fear. Raleigh was as skilled as a bottom as he was as a cocksucker. His ass wasn't tight; it was firm, but it quivered when I rammed deep. He could manipulate his ass tunnel. As I pushed in he relaxed, then tightened up as I pulled out, massaging my cock. It was great.

I was stroking his cock as I fucked, his ass began to spasm and I knew he was ready to shoot. I rammed him hard six or seven times and I went over the edge. Raleigh shot his load all over his hairy chest. The white cum stood out on his dark skin. I pulled out and added my own cum to the mess.

You never know how much cum you will shoot, or how far it will go. It's real nice when you are playing with a guy for the first time and you shoot the mother of all loads. I got the gold medal for amount and distance. Raleigh thought I was a Superman.

I got a towel to wipe up the coating of cum, but he told me, he wanted it left. That was fine with me.

"Was it good?" I asked.

"What do you think? Damn you're good," he said. "You can improve the quality of life here. I get so sick of the steady diet of conservative politics and horny politicians. I get just as horny as the next guy and I don't even mind a little hypocrisy, but these guys are a trip. They talk about family and old fashioned, All-American, values but are trying to find a way to get a black chauffeur's cock in their ass. "

"Have you found any good recreational outlets? Can you recommend any playmates?" I asked.

"Come by the Governor's cottage tomorrow morning around ten, I've got some friends coming over. They'd love some new meat."

"Where's the Governor?"

"Golfing, lunch, and then poker. He's gone every day," Raleigh said. "Are you game?"

"I sure am," I replied. Raleigh returned to the Governor's cottage. I went to bed. I had some leads and felt as if I was a bear who had fallen into a tub of honey.

Part 4

I called into the office the next morning and there was nothing new there. Frank thought Lonnie was planning to have a hot date with his contact that afternoon. "You know, no one is better at getting all the details than Lonnie," Frank said. "He has a knack for getting information out of guys."

"I've noticed that," I said. "He seems to have the flighty, hairdresser's babble down pat. He seems so harmless."

"By the way, one of my computer nerds had a friend who just retired from the Commission for Corporations. He thinks we can get in and do some snooping," Frank added. "There seems to be corporations within corporations and we can't find the core." We talked about some office management problems and then Frank hung up.

I went out and walked around the club. I saw Charley and we talked a minute or two. He said, he would have some time that evening and might come by the athletic club. I said that was fine with me. As I walked by

Governor Johnson's cottage, Raleigh spotted me and waved at me to come in.

"I really enjoyed last night," he said. "You may not have guessed, but I'm not exactly a virgin. You are fucking hot in bed."

"Some of my friends accuse me of being a cum hound and letting my cock do my thinking for me," I confessed. "Everyone has to have a hobby, I guess and that's mine. I sure don't mind ringing your bells. I'm a confirmed top."

"Me too, last night was an exception," Raleigh said. "I don't believe I enjoyed it so much."

"To tell you the truth, I was thinking I might like a ride on your baby maker," I said. The doorbell rang. Raleigh answered it and returned with a tall young man.

"Will, this is CW, he's the night manager," We shook hands. The doorbell rang again. This time Raleigh returned with two men. One was a short, but very muscular black man named Jefferson. He was a waiter. The other man was a big, beefy, black haired bear named Louie. He was in charge of the golf carts. Raleigh introduced everyone. They were all acquainted, except for CW and me.

"I hope you guys don't mind, but some of you've got to work this afternoon. Let's get acquainted while we get naked," Raleigh said as we went to Raleigh's bedroom and got down to business.

I hate to sound superficial, but there are times when it's nice to get together with some guys for plain old sex. No conversation or getting to know each other, just sex. This was one of those times. Everyone was here for the same reason.

"I'm new here," CW said as he stripped, "Is anything out of bounds? Is this all oral?"

"It's been all sucking in the past," Raleigh replied, "but I've got no problem with ass play, as you all know well. Does anyone object?"

"Are you kidding?" Jefferson said.

"Shit no!" Louie said. "And if anyone is interested, I'm about as versatile as a guy can get. I like it any and every way I can get it, or give it,"

CW laughed. "I'm not that versatile," CW said, "but ask me again in another hour or so!" We were all naked by now and my cock had begun to work its magic. I have no illusions as to my attractiveness, but my cock is a stud magnet. Before I had a chance to decide who to play with, Jefferson was at my cock. CW was worshiping at Raleigh's shrine and Louie came over to me and we hugged.

I hate to sound superficial, but I love it when you meet strangers, get naked and hard and then go at it like dogs in heat. Sometimes it's nice to find out who is with the program and willing to play right off the bat. The small talk between meeting a guy and having sex with him is always uncomfortable for me. I was never good at bar talk. You seem to be dancing around the subject and pretending to be interested in the guy's personality.

To tell the truth, I am interested in a personality. I really dislike guys with attitude. I don't like "Bad Boy" types or role players. I have no desire to play Daddy or Cop. I have discovered you can find out more about a man's personality after I've played cock tag with his prostate and you've both drained your balls. Sometimes an ass filled with my sperm is the perfect cure for attitude problems.

Jefferson didn't mind having a second cock within sucking distance at all. Jefferson was shaved, with only a tuft of hair in his pubic region. His cut cock was long with a big mushroom head on a thin shaft. It was so hard it curved back to touch his navel. My cock is thick, but Louie's was a genuine fireplug, fat and stumpy. Jefferson liked each.

As he sucked, Jefferson arranged himself so he was on his hands and knees. Jefferson's ass was in the air and spread, exposing his hole. Raleigh noticed that and he and CW came over to join us. I saw CW's cock was already glistening with lube. CW got behind Jefferson and positioned his cock head at the black man's ass.

"I'm going to do this nice and easy so you can still service that monster cock you're nursing on," CW said. "Nice and easy." CW was well equipped. He was a bit thicker and longer than average and had low hanging balls dangling under his erect meat. He popped his cock into Jefferson's ass and Jefferson didn't miss a lick. As CW slipped his cock deeper into his ass, Jefferson purred.

"Shit, that looks like fun," Louie said. Raleigh looked at him and I knew what was next. Soon, Louie was on his knees, getting ready to take it doggy style. Jefferson remained cool and collected as CW massaged his insides. There was nothing cool and collected about Raleigh fucking Louie. It was hot, sweaty, man sex.

Raleigh was about as big as Louie could take, so it didn't fit easily. It took some forcing, and Louie didn't mind some work as long as Raleigh got every inch of his cock embedded in his ass. Louie was moaning as Raleigh finally got the entire cock into Louie's ass. Raleigh moved on to the deep thrusting phase. He pulled out all of the way, leaving only the cock head in the hole, and then he jammed it in. Poor Louie loved it.

CW was fucking Jefferson in such a gentlemanly way; I decided to see if I could get CW a bit hot and bothered. I was rock hard after Jefferson's sucking, so I went to CW's rear and nosed my cock into his ass. He didn't expect the visit in the rear, but it wasn't unwelcome. He adjusted his position to make it easier to enter. Raleigh handed me a tube of lubricant and I coated my cock with a thick coat.

I popped my cock head into his hole again. There was some resistance, but nothing out of the usual. I pushed again. He opened wide and my entire cock vanished up CW's shit tunnel in a single movement.

"Holy shit! What in hell is that?" CW cried. I pulled out most of the way and shoved it in deep again. I must have winded him that time. He had barely glanced at me when I undressed and my cock had been in Jefferson's gullet ever since. CW hadn't realized how big I was. I slowly pumped for a while until CW got his breath back. As he relaxed, I began to pump harder and deeper. CW began to twitch and moan.

"Whatever you are doing, keep it up!" Jefferson cried. "It's great! It feels like your cock is growing!" Apparently my cock in CW's ass gave him a boost. I could feel Jefferson undulating his ass as he tried to get CW's cock deeper. I began deep thrusting; both Jefferson and CW lost it. For a few minutes it was the perfect double fuck. We rhythmically undulated, cocks and asses rubbing and sliding in unison.

I didn't think it could get much better, but I felt a cock at my ass. Louie was on the floor scooting under Jefferson so he could suck the black man's cock. Raleigh was knocking at my back door. I figured what the hell; I'm nothing if not a good sport. I shifted my legs and opened up.

Raleigh was considerate, but insistent. His cock was big, but not quite as big as my friend Mark's. It stretched and filled me. I never know how a cock will feel in my ass. Raleigh had a good cock, but his cock head was great. He rubbed his knob against my prostate as I did the same to CW

CW was tall and I was having a problem staying in his ass. When Raleigh fucked me he solved the problem. His cock was thick enough to support me. I was the filling in a fuck sandwich. My knees didn't touch the floor sometimes, especially when Raleigh was thrusting deep.

I liked Raleigh, but my prostate fell in love with his cock head. I began to lose it. We all merged into a single fucking mass of cocks and assholes. Jefferson popped first. He was 69ing with Louie. Louie started to moan as he loudly slurped up Jefferson's cum. Louie then shot off like a Roman candle. His fireplug sprayed and spurted cum in every direction.

The feel of the warm cum splashing on our bodies did nothing to cool things down. CW started quickly jerking his ass and I knew he was

41

rear loading Jefferson. I could feel his ass contracting on my cock as he ejaculated. That was enough for me. I let go and just let it fly.

Raleigh was still thrusting. I'm not sure I had ever had an orgasm while a guy fucked me. It was good. When I finally stopped shooting, I felt like a wet dishrag. Raleigh was still fucking and I relaxed as the last drops of cum drained from my cock.

"That's it!" Raleigh cried. "That feels great." He made a half dozen more thrusts and he popped. We finally broke apart. When I pulled out of CW, my sperm dribbled out of his ass. It had been a big load.

"Shit, guys, was that as hot as it seemed to me?" CW asked.

"It seemed that way to me," I said. "You've got cum drooling from your ass, you'd better shower."

"I feel warm all over," Louie said. "I've never done anything this hot before. I need a shower too. I've got to get back to my stable of golf chariots."

"Feeding time?" Raleigh asked.

"Yes. You'd think adult men could plug in the things, but it's too much for most of the club members," Louie explained. "It's as if they'd die trying to help." We didn't all fit in the shower, so I talked with Jefferson and Raleigh, while CW and Louie showered first.

"I don't mind the old men, it's the young guys I hate," Jefferson said. "How do guys that young get so pompous? It takes your breath away."

"Wilton?" I asked.

"That's him and his harem," Jefferson said, confirming my guess. "He's almost as rude as the Governor. He won't even say hello, unless you have ten thousand to invest."

"Is that the price of admission?" I asked.

"That's the way it seems to me. That and a blow job," Jefferson replied. "I guess you can tell, I'm no prude, but sex for money turns me off."

"You think that's what's going on?" I asked.

"I do room service for three nights a week, I know who's sleeping with whom," he said. "These old codgers think they've hit the jackpot with a young virgin stud that's attracted to them and is willing to put out. These boys are young, but they're used." Lou and C.W finished their showers and Jefferson and I replaced them in the bathroom.

In the shower, I was shocked to discover I was still horny. I looked at Jefferson and saw he was in the same state.

"I think there's enough lube left in my ass to make it pretty easy," he said as he looked at my erection.

"I'm big."

"Why do you think I'm here?" Jefferson said, as he bent over. "I love uncut cock." He had a velvet ass. It was odd feeling, but very sensual. He was tight, but offered no resistance, other than friction. Once I was in deep, his ass seemed to bond to my skin. His ass held the skin tight, but since I'm uncut, my shaft and head fucked inside the skin tube. It was great. I pulled out after a while and bent over to give him a trip in my ass. As with Raleigh earlier, his cock head was great.

"Is that lube, or Raleigh's cum that makes it so smooth in there?" he asked.

"I don't know, but I'll bet its fifty/ fifty," I said. "Is it good?" Jefferson suddenly began to pump wildly. He was shooting again. He stopped just as suddenly.

43

"Sorry about that," he said, "I usually ask before I shoot." I stood up. His cock popped out of my ass.

"Shooting off is the name of the game isn't it?" I remarked. We cleaned up and I went to the club and work.

Jason arrived earlier in the afternoon than on the previous days and was talking to another older man. Mr. Donovan was a Texas oil man, visiting Washington to put some pressure on the Department of Energy. He was loud and pushy. He was also in better shape than many of the other members of the club. He was a good 6'-4", with black hair and the remains of a physique. He had been a college football star and made sure you knew it.

My role as the perfect servant made it possible to circulate around the room and listen in on the conversations. Half of the conversations were about golf, or the condition of the greens. Most of the rest were about business or politics. My predecessor in the job had been a black man. Most of the men were relieved to have a white guy taking the job. It let them be a bit more direct in their expressions about racial issues.

Donovan had very clear ideas on that subject, mostly of the "send them back to Africa" variety. Jason held a similar opinion. Jason was a good bull shitter and he was shoveling on the shit for Donovan. Donovan did have a bit of the Marlboro man look, plus 30 pounds. He also packed quite a basket. He exercised very vigorously and poor Jason had a hard time keeping up.

They showered together and went to the steam room. Donovan looked a bit uncomfortable and glanced around before he went in. He didn't want anyone to see him. I went in about ten minutes later on one of my inspection tours. Jason left as I entered.

"Anyone leave any towels in here?" I asked.

"No, why do you care?" Donovan asked, clearly annoyed.

"One of the guests lost his keys earlier," I said. "He usually pins it to his towel. I thought he might have left it here." My eyes had adapted to the steamy room. He was sitting in the far corner. A towel covered what remained of his erection. "Do you need anything?" I asked.

"What I need, you can't give me," he said, as he stood up to leave. His towel fell off and I saw his half erect cock. It was a nice piece of meat. I'm afraid he caught my admiring glance.

"I'm going to block open the door and hose it down in here before the evening crowd. Do you mind?"

Donovan muttered, no, and left the room.

Part 5

Charley exercised after dinner, but he was with several other men and a poker game was in the works. He left for the game and the exercise area was empty. Governor Johnson returned, as did Jason. The elderly man was clearly infatuated with the young man.

Johnson knew the young man was Jason when he arrived, but after a half hour, Jason had become Jimmy, his long dead son. The Governor was beaming in pleasure. In his confused mind, the death had just been a dream. The old man was a first class asshole when he was with it. As he slipped into the confused state he turned into a doting father. Jason played it to the hilt.

Donovan returned and wasn't at all pleased to see Jason with Governor Johnson. I don't think it was jealousy. Donovan looked as if he realized what Jason was and understood the game the boy was playing. Another man joined Donovan and they exercised. Hal was Donovan's age, but in average shape. It was clear Hal admired the more muscular man. Hal complimented Donovan on his good physical condition and was talking about getting back into shape again.

Hal was in his early 60s, about six feet tall and 230 pounds. He had a close-cropped beard and chest hairs poked above his tee shirt. He seemed cheerful and kept a conversation going with Donovan. Donovan liked the open admiration showered on him by Hal, so he was civil and pleasant. Wandering by, I heard Donovan say, "I've got this problem in the DOE, do you have some connections there?"

Hal said, "Sure, I know a few guys at the "assistant to" level. That's where all the real work is done." I wandered off, but that helped to explain Donovan's good attitude. He wanted something from Hal.

Wilton came in. He said hello to Hal, but joined the Governor and Jason. I didn't know enough about the scam as yet, but I had a suspicion the two young men were reeling the Governor in. Hal looked a bit surprised Wilton hadn't come over to join him. Maybe disappointed is a better way to describe Hal's look.

Jason and Wilton showered with the Governor and I overheard them talking about going to his cottage afterward for a nightcap. I saw the three of them in the shower. Wilton was tanned and toned, but not muscular. He had a nice body; a compact set of balls and cock. Jason was pale. He was healthy, but never got into the sun. He was hairless, except for his pubic bush. His soft cock was five inches of thick meat and had potential.

The Governor was an overweight, old man in poor physical condition. Skin and fat seemed to hang from him. The contrast between him and the two other men was striking and unsettling. It was easy to understand the attraction the elderly man felt for Jason and Wilton. For their part, Jason and Wilton looked at the Governor as a cash cow. I felt a twinge of pity for him.

They went off to the Governor's cottage. Donovan was next in the showers. Hal joined him a minute or two later. Donovan was handsome and very much aware of how handsome he was. He was perfectly groomed and I suspected he trimmed his body hair to keep it even. He was nicely hung.

Hal was a shaggy dog type. Not a hair on his head, chest, back or gut was in place, or ever had they been in place. His body wasn't in bad shape, but it wasn't good either. He was a typical, middle-aged man who ate a bit too much and didn't exercise enough. He had a fire hose hanging between his legs. He also had huge balls in a hairy sack.

You can never completely judge a cock in its soft state. I've seen some mini cocks that turned into impressive specimens and some monsters that were six inches soft and six inches hard. Hal's was going to be a good one, I was sure. It wasn't pretty, but it was prime meat.

Donovan left and Hal went into the steam room. Much to my surprise, Charley returned. He had apparently left the poker game early and wanted to work out again. Afterwards, he showered and went into the steam room.

The place was empty now, so I closed up the exercise area and then checked out the steam room.

"Is everything okay in here?" I called as I entered to room. "Don't get overheated."

"It's fine," Charley answered. "Is that you Will?"

"It sure is," I said. I could hear Charley saying, under his breath, "Will's okay. Don't worry, he's with the program." I went deeper into the steam room and they came into view. When Charley saw me he took off the towel he had draped over his cock. He was fully erect.

"Is this a private party?" I asked.

"Not anymore!" Charley said. I bent over and sucked him.

49

"Hot damn!" cried Hal as he scooted closer. Through the steamy mist I could see his cock was everything I had guessed it would be.

"Go try him out," Charley suggested, "He's got a monster." I tried Hal's cock. It was a good seven inches, but I was able to deep throat it in spite of the size.

Hal moaned and twitched. "This guy's a real find, Charlie! Damn he's good." I came up for air.

"Let's adjourn to my bedroom where we can play without disturbance and not get cooked by the steam," I suggested. Both men were more than ready. Hal turned out to be a lot of fun. He was no newcomer to the world of man sex. Charley had relaxed some. The night before, he had been uneasy. Now he was more comfortable

We had a first rate suck session with everyone getting really into it. Charley came close to deep throating me. Hal was good about letting you know where he was in the build up to his orgasm, so you knew when to let up and let him calm down.

"Do either of you guys like to fuck?" asked Hal.

"Well, it depends if you are a top or a bottom," I answered. "I do it all, but I have to admit I have a real warm spot for the top."

"Never done it," Charley said. "I might like to try it though. Top I mean. I don't think I could bottom."

"This is your lucky night!" Hal said. "I like it all too, but I have a special place in my heart for the bottom. Will, I don't think I've taken a cock as big as yours in years. I would sure like to see if it still rings my chimes. Are you game?"

"Yep. I'm ready, willing and able," I said.

"Maybe I should go," Charley said. He didn't want to go, he just wasn't sure he wanted to watch.

"If you don't mind something educational, stay around," Hal said. "If you want, I wouldn't mind giving you a tour of the tunnel of love. I'm a bit of an exhibitionist. I like to be watched. You don't mind if Charley watches Will, do you?"

"Not at all. I got an advanced degree in fucking. Don't mind demonstrating it at all," I said, as I got some lube out of the table beside my bed. "Why don't you lie back and open up?" Hal was already on the bed. He had a hairy ass with a pink hole, centered on a little rosebud.

I spread the lubricant around his hole before I pushed the rosebud into his ass. "Damn you're tight. Are you sure you want to get fucked?" I asked.

"I said it had been a while. If you take your time, I'll be fine," Hal replied. I pressed deeper and hit his prostate. "You got it! Just hit the same spot with your cock a few times! It feels great." I coated my cock with a thick layer of lube and began to ease my way into his ass. It wasn't easy. He was just as tight as I had guessed. Fortunately, he also was willing. I turned my cock into a battering ram and eventually forced my way in.

Once I had popped through Hal's sphincter, he began to respond enthusiastically. He was just as tight for the last six inches of penetration as for the first three, but he sure enjoyed it more. Once I filled him completely, I pulled out, re-lubricated him and shoved it in again. I did this two more times. His ass was still tight, but the increased lubrication made it impossible for him to resist. My cock was continuously squeezed by Hal's tunnel. I've fucked one or two men in my day and never felt anything like Hal's ass.

After a while I let Charley try him out. Charley had been watching and marveling that my cock fit Hal's ass. Charley was still a bit shy about fucking, but I knew Hal was a true ass slut and would enjoy his cock.

After all my work, Charley slid in easily and they had a good time. Charley was really turned on and he didn't last long. He tried to pull out when he started to shoot, but I stopped him. I wanted some of his man made lube in Hal's ass for my next visit.

"I wouldn't mind another trip in your tunnel of love, if you don't mind?" I asked. Hal just smiled and nodded. I slid in easily this time, tight, but easy. Remarkably, Charley's cum oozed out from the asshole when Hal was fully impaled by my cock. He was that tight. I fucked Hal for a good ten to fifteen minutes.

"Would you mind if I took a breather?" Hal asked. "I'm feeling a bit..." I rammed him hard and pulled out. I didn't want him to be uncomfortable. Between Charley and me, we had been at it for a good 45 minutes. Remarkably, neither Hal nor I had shot off yet. Charley was almost asleep on the bed next to Hal. Hal's cock was hard as a rock and I wanted sex bad. I coated Hal's cock and straddled it.

"I thought you were a top?" Hal commented.

"90% top. Do you mind if I check out the other 10%?" I asked.

"Not one bit!" Hal replied enthusiastically. I positioned Hal's monster at my hole and sat back slowly. I'm not that experienced, but my friend Mark has a cock about the same size as Hal's and I had grown to like Mark's cock a lot. Hal's cock head was a lot bigger. I bounced on the massive member. My ass slowly stretched and finally I got the head safely into my ass. The rest was easy. Easy is not quite the right word, but it did get in.

I was resting on his pubic hairs, totally impaled. I relaxed, closed my eyes, arched my back and sort of stretched. As I relaxed Hal's cock seemed to slip into just the right spot. A wave of pleasure swept over me. I had known Hal for no more than two hours and now his cock was deep in my ass and it felt great. I began to twitch my ass. Hal and I settled down for a long session.

I was rock hard, as was Hal. There was barely enough room for his cock and my prostate in the tight hole. With my prostate squeezed, every movement I made with my hips seemed to send electric shocks of pleasure through my body.

Charley had been watching half asleep, but rallied when Hal fucked me. "Shit, I don't believe that fucker fits!" he said. "Is there any room left for your interior organs? It looks like you're getting CPR with a cock!" Just then, Hal jerked, ramming his cock deeper. I almost passed out it felt so good. "What does it feel like?" Charlie asked. "Getting fucked, I mean." I was in no condition to talk, but Hal answered.

"Every cock and every ass is different," Hal explained. "For some guys it's nothing but pain and discomfort. If your ass is really tight and the cock his really big, things just don't work out."

"But you're tight?" Charlie replied. "You didn't have any problem."

"It wasn't easy at first. I started years ago. I was much taken with an incredibly handsome stud who liked the top," Hal explained. "He was a nice guy, but he was big. We had enjoyed sucking and 69ing, but we got in a threesome once and he fucked the third. Al had told me he liked to fuck, but had never insisted, but when I saw him in action, I knew just how much he liked it."

"I figured, if I wanted to keep him, I'd better figure out how to take it and enjoy it," continued Hal. "It wasn't easy. He was a nice guy and didn't want to hurt me. Luckily, the second time he fucked me, he found the right spot and he rang my chimes. Once I figured out the objective, I was willing to work at it."

"It looks like you like it now," Charley said.

"I sure do," Hal said, "as does Will, here." He jerked again, ramming my ass and sending me to the moon. "Will likes them big. So do I for that matter. I think it's the pressure the cock exerts on the prostate that does the trick for me. I don't know exactly what's going on, but it seems to me the prostate is the stealth sex organ. Damn few guys know it's there, but it sure does the trick." Charley fed his cock to Hal. Then, much to my surprise, Charley bent over and began suck my cock.

I had been oozing precum for fifteen minutes and the taste must have gotten to Charley. He was like a four year old licking his first ice cream cone. It took about a minute of this treatment and the precum was joined by the thicker white stuff. Charley jumped back when he was hit by my scuz on the first ejaculation. He then enveloped my cock head with his lips again and took the rest of the cum, fresh as it spurted from my cock head. Charley was getting into it.

Part 6

When I called into the office the next morning a lot had happened. They said Lonnie's date had been a great success. I called Lonnie for the details.

The boy he dated was horny as hell and desperate for younger meat. Lonnie was 45 or so, but looked younger and was in good shape, not muscular, but toned. The boy, Johnny, was handsome, almost pretty. Lonnie said he was slim, with black, curly hair and a closely cropped beard. He had pale, blue eyes and clear, white skin.

"Did you like him?"I asked.

"I sure did. He wanted a father and I got to play Dad," Lonnie said. "He comes from a nice redneck family near Charlottesville, is gay as a goose and is clueless."

"What do you mean," I asked.

"He's 23. He likes sex and he likes older men. He thinks it's real."

"What's real?"

"The investment opportunity," Lonnie replied. "Johnny gets a $5,000.00 "signing fee" for each trick. Wilton told him that the fee is justified because the guys can make hundreds of thousands from investments. Wilton said it was worth it. The normal investment is $10,000.00. You don't need to be a rocket scientist to know a 50% finder fee is pretty outlandish, but I'm not sure Johnny knows that."

"Not a rocket scientist?"

"He doesn't seem to be stupid. It's not clear exactly which planet he lives on," Lonnie said. "Wilton is good in bed too. He introduced Johnny to a few parts of his anatomy the boy didn't know he had."

"Nothing new for you?" I asked, laughing.

"No, but I did turn Johnny from a bottom into a truly versatile fucker," he said. "Wilton is a believer in the "every-hair-in-its-place" school of sex. I introduced him to the wild and woolly school. The boy liked it. He liked it a lot."

"I take it you liked it too."

"Damn right," Lonnie replied. "At first I thought he was cock starved, but the boy really wants a Dad to teach him the ropes. The kid's hung too. Not like you, but a nice piece of meat none the less."

"Did you get any real information out of him, or did you just perform your fatherly duties?"

"I did it all," Lonnie replied. "I was doing the dance of lust on his cock and we talked too. Damn I like his cock."

"You can think and get fucked at the same time?" I asked.

"I sure as shit can!" he exclaimed. "Quite frankly, I need to. If I stopped thinking every time I sat on a cock, my mind would atrophy from lack of use! Anyway, Johnny said, Wilton found him at the Jamestowne Club as a waiter. Wilton has a good line, telling him he could spot talent and he had an opportunity for him. Wilton has a spectacular apartment near the club and Johnny was impressed. The kid wants to live the good life. Wilton told him, he could do just as well.

Johnny spent a weekend of "training" at Wilton's beach house and then went hunting for wealthy men. Wilton had identified some likely prospects. When Johnny met the first client, he struck pay dirt and he was hooked. He had never had that much money before.

"I'm afraid Johnnie doesn't have the makings of a good whore," Lonnie said. "He likes sex with men, but not just anyone. Wilton wanted him to bed all his clients. He told Johnny, the clients couldn't complain if they got some ass out of it too. Johnny didn't understand what that meant."

"None of the "clients" can face a scandal? It's a clever scheme," I said. "Some of them will eventually find out, but he must be betting they'd be too embarrassed to call the cops."

"That's the way it looks to me," Lonnie said. "I don't think Johnny's really with the program. Wilton's been complaining he's not been aggressive enough. Poor Johnny thinks he's selling investment opportunities, not cock."

"You like him a lot, don't you?"

"I kind of think I do. I don't think he's dumb; really inexperienced though. Johnny is getting suspicious. The money is so good; the temptation is almost too much for him. I think I got him to look beyond that."

"You didn't tell him we are investigating the operation?"

"Shit no," Lonnie answered. "But he can be helpful to us." He paused. "Have you ever been having sex with a guy when it turns from being good to being great?"

"What do you mean?"

"We had a long night. I fucked him a few times and he fucked me. I was going in for a third trip up the tunnel of love and it suddenly clicked," Lonnie explained. "I was enjoying it of course, but we merged. My cock became a part of him. I couldn't tell where I started and he ended. It was incredible. Johnny felt the same thing."

"I know what you are talking about," I said. "That happened to Mark and me once."

"Only once?" Lonnie asked. I laughed.

"No, we've hit the same spot a few more times," I said. "Not every time, but we have done it."

"I'm in fucking love!" Lonnie said.

"I'll bet it's a massive case of lust!" I said.

"It might be, but it sure felt good while we were doing it," Lonnie added. We finished the conversation. I said I would call again in a day or two.

It was a beautiful day, so all the members were golfing in a tournament. It was quiet at the clubhouse. I went walking and ran into Raleigh and Jefferson sitting on the terrace of the Governor's cottage. They were off duty while most of the guests were off playing.

"How's the Governor doing?" I asked.

"On and off," Raleigh said. "He has good days and not so good days. It's getting strange. That boy is up to something. I don't trust that man."

"Is that Jason, you're talking about?" Jefferson asked. "He's a 100%, pure asshole."

"You know him?" I asked.

"I sure as hell do. He's one of those spoiled rich kids, who thinks the world owes him something," explained Jefferson. "I don't mind the men that much; at least they worked for their money. Jason is one of those guys who think you can inherit respect. He treats everyone outside of his social class as scum."

"That's always nice in a person. Is he a hit with all of the staff?" I asked.

"Everyone thinks he's a fucking prince," Jefferson replied. He took a long look at me. "Talking about fucking, do you have some time? I'd love to get off."

"You have to forgive Jefferson," Raleigh said. "I'm afraid I've been talking to him about redneck, donkey dicks and it seems as if I've converted him to my way of thinking. I was planning to screw him, but I don't mind if you do the honors. I've been up his ass enough."

Raleigh didn't seem to know I had already been in Jefferson's ass in the shower, but I guessed Jefferson wanted it that way, so I didn't say anything. I had a suspicion Raleigh and Jefferson were closer than I thought. Jefferson was Raleigh's boy and Raleigh had to give permission.

"If you guys think I'm a cheap, slutty, redneck who would jump into bed with anyone who asks," I said, "you've figured me out pretty well. You like the bottom that much, Jefferson?"

"I guess you could say, I'm a recent convert," the young black man said. "I had cut a wide swath as a top until I met Raleigh here. I had tried a few cocks in my hole when I was a kid and they didn't do anything for me. After my experiences with Raleigh, I discovered the doorbell that rings my chimes is deeper in my shit tunnel than most guys. Ever since Raleigh rang it, I can't seem to get enough."

"I've rang the chimes the first time, but the other day, CW found the magic spot too," Raleigh explained. "We had arranged for me to do the honors again, but CW was first in line, so I let him give Jefferson a ride."

"I don't want to sound like a racist pig, but no black man ever had as little interest in being fucked by a white man than me," Jefferson added.

"Until CW's cock rammed your prostate?" I asked.

"You got it! I don't know if it was the cock, or the idea of a white cock in my ass. Whatever it was, it turned me on. Forbidden fruit maybe," Jefferson said. "I figure you've got twice the cock CW has and you must be four times more redneck..."

"So you figure I'll be at least twice as good?" I said, completing his sentence.

"Bingo!" replied Jefferson. We all went to the bedroom and stripped. Jefferson was at my cock as soon as I was naked. I nursed Raleigh's monster and we all got into the mood real fast. I had fucked Jefferson doggy style in the shower two days earlier and it had been good. CW had spent a good fifteen minutes fucking the black man and had shot his load into his ass before I got in. Jefferson's ass was as relaxed and lubricated as it could be. I have always thought man cum is the best lube and CW's load had been a prizewinner.

I had enjoyed Jefferson before, but today he seemed like another man. He was better. This time I fucked him spread-eagle style on his back with his legs spread. I was also the first to fuck him this way. He was tight and a bit tense. He didn't fight my cock, but there was enough resistance to be fun for him and me. He was muscular, toned and tightly wound.

It took some work to get my club cock through Jefferson's muscular buns, but once my cock head popped the sphincter, it was easier. His whole love tunnel was trying to grab my cock and hold it. At first I thought he was trying to keep me from going in deep, but once I was in, he still grabbed tight. When I pulled out, he had actually pulled my foreskin over my cock head. He was grabbing that tight.

Needless to say, I shoved it right in again. His hole peeled back the skin and exposed the head as it penetrated his ass. My cockhead gets sensitive when I fuck and his ass lining was rubbing the sensitive gland. I was really enjoying myself. Raleigh was watching and smiling in approval. When I pulled out the next time, Jefferson again pulled the skin over the head.

I shoved in fast the next time. Jefferson and Raleigh both moaned in approval. This time Jefferson twitched and shot a single glob of cum on his chest.

"Are you shooting?" I asked. "I can hold back some if you want me too. I'd love for this to last longer."

"Just keep on doing what you're doing. I can control it," Jefferson said. I didn't believe him, but he was right. He had a slow motion orgasm. He ejaculated a single shot every fourth or fifth stroke of my cock. We fucked for a good ten minutes and he never shot more than one glob at a time and he never was more than a half second from a total orgasm the whole time. I would hold back a little after each ejaculation; I didn't want to press my luck. I could tell when he dropped just below the threshold and began thrusting again.

"Shit, Jeffy baby, you've been holding out on me," Raleigh exclaimed. "When did you learn to do that?"

"I've been working on mind and muscle control," Jefferson replied. I know how good it feels the seconds before an orgasm. Jefferson spent a good ten minutes in that state. "Could you do one thing, Will?" He asked, "When you cum, pull out and shoot it all over me. I'd love that."

"No problem, anything you want," I said. I was in good shape too, rock hard and excited, but I knew I wasn't going to cum right away. Jefferson let loose another shot. His cock was bent toward his navel and each glob of cum landed in a straight line, as if he was marking the white lines on a highway. Raleigh was behind me. He was a lot taller than me, so he was looking over my shoulder. I felt the warm spray of man seed on my back.

"Sorry about that," Raleigh said. "I got a bit excited." As I said, I had been in good shape holding back, but the warm cum running down the small of my back was too much. I pulled out and my cock exploded. Jefferson had shot a neat line of semen. I shot randomly all over him. His smooth, defined muscles looked as if someone had dropped a gallon of cum paint all over him. There were big globs, little sprays and trails of cum from his chest to his bush.

Raleigh looked at the display in clear admiration. Jefferson lost control as I shot off and he finished his orgasms with multiple ejaculations. It was hard to believe there was anything left in his balls, by that time. I got on the bed, wiped out. Raleigh straddled me and fed me his cock. He was still drooling cum and I sucked what remained out of his dick. He leaned over and sucked Jefferson's still throbbing cock. He was at the tail end of his climax, but when his lips touched Jefferson's cock, Raleigh shot a big glob of cum. Cocks don't lie and Raleigh liked Jefferson a lot. We cleaned up and got back to work.

Part 7

The golf tournament ended with a Banquet and Awards Ceremony, so there was almost no one at the exercise area that night. I had my first sex free night since I had started working at the club. It was nice to have a good night's sleep. I woke rested and ready to go. I called the office to get the latest news. I got Butch, one of the founders of Clydesdale & Company.

"All hell broke loose here," Butch reported. "Magnus is dead. It's all over the paper."

"What happened?"

"Automobile accident on River Road, you know the bad turn near the Nickel Bridge. He apparently went off the road," Butch explained. "I don't like it, something smells."

"What do you mean?" I asked.

"No one seems to have any idea why he was there. His house is in the deepest West End. He had no reason to be on the other side of the river. John says he was a careful driver."

"Is this in the paper?" I asked.

"Hell no. The paper is all "Tragic Accident claims Philanthropist"", Butch explained. "John called the servants to get the inside scoop. They were real unhappy and think something is afoot." John is my contractor friend who set me up in business. John was a steady and sensible man, not an alarmist at all. I decided to call John and get the details. I called him, but he was out, so I left a message and asked him to call me back.

I called Colin, the art collector whose friend had committed suicide. He was home. The butler said he wasn't receiving calls. I asked him to give Colin my number. The Butler reluctantly agreed to do so. A minute later my phone rang. It was Colin.

"Thank God you called!" he exclaimed. "It's awful! Poor Magnus. I'm sure they did him in! The police say it's an accident. I don't believe that for a second! He was a dear man! You could always count on him" Colin was talking a mile a minute. His voice was breaking with emotion when he spoke of Magnus. We talked for a while and he calmed down some. At first I thought he was just hysterical, but as I talked it became clear he had some reason to be suspicious.

"Magnus was afraid his contact was getting suspicious. He had been stringing him along," Colin said.

"Who was his contact?" I asked.

"A boy named Temple. An Archangel School alumnus, Magnus didn't like him much. Temple was either servile, or demanding. It was a hard combination to deal with," Colin explained. "Magnus was wondering if there was something mentally wrong with the kid. I told him to break it off. Magnus, as you know, wasn't that kind of man. He was a bloodhound hot on the trail."

"The boy had a split personality?"

"I'm not sure it was that serious, but Magnus was uncomfortable," Colin said. "The Police say, it was poorly maintained brakes. There's no chance in hell that's the case. Have you ever met Hans, the chauffeur? He treated those cars like his children. They were in perfect condition."

"He drove a Mercedes, didn't he?"

"Yes, Hans is an Auto-Nazi. He didn't let dust settle on the car, let alone allow the brakes go bad," Colin said. "Embezzlement is bad enough. Murder is..." Colin couldn't finish the sentence.

"We're on the case," I said. "The Police are on the job, they may solve it."

"For some reason, State Troopers are on the job. It should be a City Police case," Colin said.

"This is puzzling," I said. We talked a bit longer and Colin hung up. None of my staff would go to the funeral; I didn't want anyone to know we were interested. Before he hung up, Colin told me cost was no object. I told Colin we would stay on the job. I called Lonnie to see if he had any information. He wasn't home.

I went to work at the exercise room. It was a busy day. Many of the men had overdone it at the banquet the night before and guilt brought them to the exercise room. The Governor was there, as was Charley. Jason arrived with a friend. I was busy with the club members and I wasn't able to get near the new guy that afternoon.

There was a break for dinner, but a few guys showed up afterward. An older man, named George, appeared and I spent a lot of time with him. He had been exhausted and winded after playing golf the day before and realized he was out of shape. Jason and his friend appeared and attached themselves to him like a leach.

I wondered if Jason had reeled in the Governor and was looking for a new conquest. The two young men were giving George advice on exercise and I realized they knew shit about exercise. I overheard Jason saying, "No pain no gain". Not a good idea for an older man just starting. I kept close to see what else they were up too.

"Hey, Temple, can you get me a towel?" Jason asked. "Georgie here needs a dry one." Thank God I had my back to them when I overheard this. My mouth dropped open. Temple must have left Richmond as soon as Magnus was dead. I wanted to take a long hard look at the boy, but I held off. I went to check the shower, steam and sauna.

When I got back, George was obviously pleased by the attention the two young men paid to him. Temple was handsome in a beach bunny like way. He was blond and bland, with pale blue eyes and a tanning salon complexion. His body was hairless and rather boyish. I assumed he shaved it. I knew Magnus' taste in men. He preferred more masculine men. Temple wasn't his type at all.

Temple was playing the eager to please servant-in-waiting. Colin had used the word "servile" and that fit him perfectly. The trio went off to the showers and I assumed to the steam room. Donovan entered the exercise area. He looked mad and undertook an extremely vigorous series of exercises.

Ten minutes later Jason left the steam room, leaving George alone with Temple. I was trying to figure out how to get in the steam room and listen in on Temple's spiel when I heard a crash in the exercise area. I ran over and found Donovan lying on the floor, under the weights. Donovan must have slipped. His arms were pinned and he was trapped and frightened. He was having problems breathing.

I was able to lift one end of the weight just enough for him to get out. Donovan had always been an asshole, but he was shaken and almost human.

"Are you okay?" I asked. "We have a doctor on call." He was gasping for breath. "Can you calm down?" He took a big breath and began breathing normally.

"I think I'm okay," he said after a few breaths. "It just scared me. I felt as if it was crushing my chest." He was silent for a minute or so. "Damn I was stupid. I should never have done that without a spotter. I should never have tried 250 pounds. How in hell did you lift it?"

"Shit, if I had known it was 250 pounds, I never would have tried," I said. He laughed.

"I'm sure glad you did," Donovan admitted. "There must be more to you than meets the eye."

"I love you too," I said.

"Sorry, I didn't mean for it to sound that way. I'm not the most diplomatic guy in the world," he replied. "I was preoccupied. One of those kids that hang around here hit on me to invest is some scheme. He gave me a name of the reference. I called up the guy and found out he was dead. The guy who answered the phone seemed to think I might have had something to do with it. It's strange. He gave me the name last night after the banquet, I call this morning and the guy is dead."

"Quite a coincidence," I said.

"Have you noticed those kids hanging around the older men?" he asked.

"I guess I have. I must not be old enough, or rich enough for them to pay any attention to me," I answered. He looked me in the eye. He had noticed the same things.

"I like sex as much as any guy, but this business deal-blow job combination gives me the willies," he said. "I'm no shrinking violet when it comes to business techniques, but I have limits."

"Do you know what the price is?" I asked.

"It seems the entrance fee is around $10,000.00," Donovan said.

"Pretty stiff price for a blow job," I commented, thinking out loud. "Shit, there are a lot of guys who would do that for free." Donovan burst out laughing.

"Hell, for ten thousand, I would do it," he said. He was joking, but I got odd vibes from the comment. "I'd hate to think I had to pay for it." I asked him again if he was feeling all right. He said he was, so I went off to the showers to clean up and see how George and Temple were doing.

They were in the shower. I didn't like George's color at all. He had been in the steam room too long. A drip of cum oozed from his cock. Temple was a fast mover. When Temple saw me he left.

"Are you okay?" I asked George. He wasn't reacting. It was an instant replay of the incident of several days earlier. I was beginning to feel like a nurse. I realized this was well beyond my expertise, so, I got him to sit down and called the Club nurse. She called the Club's Doctor. He was a member and was in the dining room. They arrived in a minute or two. George had a heart condition and was on serious, big time medication. They got him to his room and gave him a shot.

I realized Wilton's boys may have been looking for a cash cow, but they didn't seem to care if the cow died. This was the second time one of their victims almost died in the steam room. Killing the cash cow seemed like a poor business approach to me. A common whore might not feel any affection for his customer, but from a strictly business point of view you would want to keep him alive. There was something wrong with Wilton's business model.

The next morning I discovered this event reinforced the club members' view of me as a guardian angel. The manager actually came over to me, and then thanked me for my attentiveness to the members' needs. I called my office, but Butch had nothing new to report. Everyone available was on the case, but had not reported back. I went over to the Governor's cottage and told Raleigh to be careful about the Governor's safety. He laughed.

"Do you really think those twinks would do something?" he asked.

"Yes," I said. "Some very odd things are going on. And keep an eye on his check book."

"How do you know this?" Raleigh asked.

"Let's just say I've got some connections," I answered. He looked at me closely.

"I've always got my eyes open," he said.

There was a big meeting in Washington coming up next week and the club had another golf tournament on the weekend. This would give congressmen and lobbyists an informal chance to get together casually in advance of the conference. The Club was all white, all male and all Republican, so you were sure to meet only sensible people here. That and have a fling with a 20 year old "investment advisor". The Club was so safe none would have guessed what Wilton and his boys were up to.

New people were arriving all day long and I was busy playing towel boy. I saw some faces I recognized as congressmen, but most of the people were congressional aides or Assistant to the Secretary Type people. These were the men who did the work behind the scenes.

The exercise room was busy after dinner. The portion of the group into fitness needed to recover after a big dinner and lots of drinking. Apparently the exercise room was thought to be a good place to sober up. Donovan came by with a friend, who he introduced as Henry. Henry was the assistant to a Senator, very handsome and a body builder. They had just met and seemed to hit it off. Charley and Hal came by. They wanted to exercise and then play. At least, that's what Charley said to me as he entered. All had been drinking and were much more laid back than usual.

Donovan was all but drooling over Henry. Henry seemed like a nice guy, who appreciated the attention given him by the handsome older man. As they talked and pressed weights, they both seemed to like what they saw in the other. Hal was watching them and smiling. He had been attracted to Donovan and hadn't gotten to first base. Hal came over to me.

"I must not be his type," he whispered. "But at least he has good taste in beef. Henry is an A-number-1, Choice piece of man flesh unless my eyes deceive me."

"Looks damn good to me," I said. "Who is he?"

"Henry Towbridge, aide to Senator Baldridge."

"That Conservative asshole? The Pope of the Senate?" I asked. Baldridge was a 19th century, Victorian blue stocking. He was a hundred years out of date and damn proud of it. He didn't like working men, women's rights and least of all gays. He liked Guns, God and Oil. That was about it. Which God he worshiped wasn't clear. Whoever it was, it had nothing to do with the love your neighbor god.

"That's him. He surrounds himself with handsome young, unmarried men. Insists they stay virgin until they find the right woman," Hal said with a smile.

"It looks to me like it may be a while before Henry finds the right woman," I said. Henry and Donovan were obviously much taken with each other.

"I think you're right. Henry's a good man. Reason and intelligent discussion does play a role in his thought processes. You can't say that about his boss," Hal said. "I have a feeling Henry's problem is lack of experience, not I.Q.". He paused. "If Donovan gets his way, Henry will get more experienced."

It had reached closing time. I announced the exercise area was closing. Everyone other than my friends had gone to their rooms. I cleaned up the exercise area and the locker area. I glanced into the shower area from the lockers. I realized Donovan and Henry hadn't seen each other naked before. Both were fully equipped and looked satisfied. I also caught Henry glancing at Hal's horse cock. I know a size queen when I see one.

I locked the doors and turned out the lights in the exercise room when I finished up the cleaning. Then I got back to the showers and saw the four men had adjourned to the steam room. I had to hose down the shower area with a mild disinfectant. I striped down to my shorts and gave the room a good cleaning. My experience with shower rooms was closely associated with athletes' foot. So far, the showers were free of the fungus and I was going to keep it that way.

Hal peeked out of the steam room. "Are we the only ones here?" he asked.

"Yes, I've locked up the rest of the place," I said.

"Come in and join us," Hal said. "There's room for another."

"As soon as I finish this," I replied. "Is everyone with the program in there?" Hal came into the shower room and walked over to me.

"They will be. Everyone is waiting for the starting gun!" he whispered. "Henry's not experienced, but he sure knows what he likes. Another eight or nine inches of cock will push him over the edge." Hal returned to the steam room. I finished up, put the hose away and went into the steam room.

The sexual tension and excitement level in the room was so thick you could have cut it with a knife.

"Do you mind if I join you men?" I asked.

"Not at all," Donovan said. I was surprised he was the one to invite me; I had expected Hal or Charley. "But you're a bit over dressed." I was wearing shorts only. They were in towels.

"That's a problem easy enough to solve," I said, as I stripped off my shorts. I was soft, but just enough excited to make my cock look huge.

"Damn!" Henry said. Donovan removed his towel revealing his cock. It was slightly beyond half-staff. The other men followed Donovan's lead. Henry was hard; the other men were getting close.

"Shit, it looks like I've got some catching up to do," I said. Hal bent over and began to suck Charley's cock. Donovan went after Henry.

Henry was on the marble bench, with Donovan on knees on the floor. I got up on the bench and straddled Henry with my cock dangling in his face.

"I've never sucked a cock before," Henry said, a bit uncertainly. "You're uncut."

"Well, you're starting at the top," I said. I had correctly guessed Henry was a size queen and my donkey dong was too much for him to resist. He nibbled on the skin, and then sucked it into his mouth. His tongue worked its way into the pucker and he licked my cock head. My slit was just inside and I had been oozing some. The second Henry tasted my cock jelly, he lost all inhibitions. Henry became a confirmed cocksucker.

Donovan moaned at the same time. I wasn't sure, but I had a feeling Henry's cock juices had begun to flow too. Donovan may have been new to man sex, but he knew what precum meant. Men can get an erection at the drop of a hat. They can also pretend to be interested. You can't fake precum. When Donovan tasted Henry's cock juice, he knew the younger man was into it.

Part 8

I think, deep in his heart, Donovan was straight. Henry just turned him on. It was one of those situations when you are physically attracted to someone of the same sex. Henry was both handsome and a nice guy. I know some gay men who are attracted to a particular woman. That may have been Donovan's case. It's sort of an odd situation, but Donovan was a sexual man and he also was horny as hell. Once he started, he wasn't shy and he didn't seem to have any problem dealing with Henry's cock.

I broke away from Henry. He was a gifted amateur and he was revving me up. I didn't want to shoot off too early. As I got down, I looked a Donovan. He glanced up and his eyes met mine. He looked embarrassed for a second, and then gave me a "what the hell" look and went back to nursing Henry's cock. Hal and Charley were going at it like dogs in heat on the other side of the steam room.

"If you guys would like a cooler place to play, my room's next door. Sex is a lot better without heat prostration," I suggested.

"That sounds good to me," Hal said.

"I'm not sure..," Henry said. I realized he was uncomfortable admitting he was having sex with men. In the steam room you could pretend it was just a chance encounter. If he went to my bedroom, he had to admit he wanted sex.

One of the nice things about shower room sex is that all signs of sex are automatically cleaned up. Excited cocks drip, drool and spurt. The running water takes care of all of that. All trace of sexual activity vanishes down the drain. It's easy to pretend nothing happened. In a bedroom, you can't be that neat. Precum drips and drools on the sheets and carpet. I've had to wipe off the ceiling a few times. Bedroom sex is different from shower room sex.

I have no particular theoretical problem with sperm covered sheets. I do have an utilitarian problem. I've woken up a few times glued to the sheets by my playmate's cum. The idea was good, but I'm a hairy guy. It was painful getting unstuck, sort of like natures own waxing treatment. Dried sperm is a bitch to get out of body hair.

I wasn't sure Henry was ready to go to the bedroom. "We're all big boys here and you are among friends," I said. "You've gone this far, you might as well relax and enjoy it."

"I'm afraid I've gone too far," he said a bit uncertainly.

Hal laughed. "I know what's too far and believe me, you're not even close. I'll tell you if you've gone too far!" We all went to my room. Henry did get into the swing of things. We all ganged up on him. I was on my bed holding him in my arms. Donovan was at his cock, sucking and licking. Hal and Charley flanked us and caressed Henry and his tits. When Donovan got tired, Hal replaced him at Henry's cock. Hal sucked first the cock, then the balls and finally spread Henry's legs and rimmed him.

The second Hal's tongue licked Henry's ass, his cock doubled in size. Henry was nicely hung, but he turned downright impressive as Hal's tongue worked its way into his ass. Donovan noticed this immediately and launched himself at Henry's cock again. He deep throated it just in time for Henry to erupt. It was a beautiful climax. Henry shook and quivered with each ejaculation.

Donovan was a good sport about Henry's man seed, eating it all. When the ejaculations stopped Donovan stood up and displayed a spectacular erection. His cock was respectable and attractive. I took one glance at it and I knew it was as hard as it ever would be. I was still holding Henry and wanted to give him a soft landing. Hal was now licking Henry's cock, doing cleanup service.

Charley went to Donovan and sucked him. It only took three licks and Donovan came. Donovan gave a good imitation of Mount St. Helen's having an eruption. He was frozen, with all of his energy concentrated in his cock. I had never seen so much cum shoot from a cock. People joke about buckets of cum. Donovan came as close as any man to making that phrase literally true.

Charley was fairly new to man sex and I wasn't sure how he would react to being given a sperm bath. He took it well. He didn't eat it, but he seemed to like being covered with Donovan's cum.

The party broke up. Henry and Donovan were drained. Charley must have cum in the excitement of the other men's orgasms. I hadn't noticed, but they were more relaxed than they could have been without an orgasm. They all went to their rooms. I went to bed.

It was five in the morning when someone knocked on my door. It was Henry. I asked him in.

"I'm sorry. I didn't mean to make a spectacle of myself," he said. "I've never done that before."

"You didn't make a spectacle of yourself. I enjoyed helping out and enjoyed getting you off," I said, "Shit, we're all men. We all know what it's like to shoot a load. Frankly, it was a turn on. Was it as good as it looked?"

"Yes. You're wrong when you said guys know what it's like when you shoot a load. Nothing I've ever done has come within a hundred miles of what happened last night," Henry added. "It was just that..."

"Henry, can you tell me what you really thought?" I asked. "Don't tell what you think you should have felt." Henry looked me in the eye with a sheepish expression on his face.

"I never enjoyed anything as much in my life. I didn't know you could feel that much," he whispered. I smiled. "I should be feeling guilty. That's what they say at church. Maybe I'll feel that later, but now it was just too good" he continued.

"I've been waiting for the guilt to hit, but it's been a good twenty-five or thirty years since I discovered man sex. If I'm going to feel guilty about enjoying myself, it's sure been a long time coming," I said.

He laughed. "You think it's okay?"

"Damn, I know it's great!" I replied. He said thank you and went back to his room. I went back to bed. A half hour later there was another knocking at my door. This time it was Donovan.

"Can I talk to you?" he asked. I let him in. I was becoming the Dear Abby of the resort.

"I owe you an apology," he said "You're a cock sucker, aren't you?"

"I sure as hell am," I said, "and ass fucker and man lover."

"I've been treating guys like you like dirt for years. I try it once and damn if I didn't like it," he confessed. "I thought you guys were all effeminate. You seem like regular guys."

"I am a regular guy. But, frankly, if I was a Queen of Heaven hairdresser or florist, it wouldn't be any different," I said. "You really fell strongly for Henry, didn't you?

"I guess I did," he said.

"I wouldn't worry too much about that," I said, and then I told him my theory about guys sometimes being attracted to a particular man. He looked at me a long time. He looked at my face, and then his gaze dropped to my crotch. I was wearing a robe, which had fallen open. Donovan got on his knees and took my cock into his mouth. About five minutes later his mouth was filled with my man seed. I hadn't shot off the night before, so I did myself proud. He was impressed.

"You think maybe it's not only Henry you're attracted too?" I asked after he swallowed for the third time and I finally stopped ejaculating.

He smiled. "I don't know about you, but I'm sure I like your cock."

"Well, that's a start," I said, taking it as a compliment. "Have you reloaded?"

He nodded. I returned the favor. It took a good long while for Donovan to pop a second time, but it was a good time for both of us. It was after dawn and Donovan returned to his cottage and I got a little sleep.

The conference started that day in Washington and most of the guests vanished. I had the next two days off, so I drove to Richmond to see what was going on in the investigation. I got back to the office and had a message from John. At lunch I wandered over to his house. He was home and asked me in. He had company.

"Clydesdale, I'd like you to meet Hector Bullock; he's a Professor at the University," John said in introduction. Bullock was a tall, distinguished looking man, middle aged with a bushy, but well groomed, gray beard.

"You are the famous Clydesdale?" he said in a deep voice. "I've heard a great deal about you."

"Don't believe all of it!" I said. He laughed.

"If only half is true, you've done a great deal for the city," he replied. "I was in the Art Building when the bomb blew. Catching those bastards who did it made me sleep better." We talked for a while and it became clear to me Hector was more than John's casual friend. The conversation turned to Magnus' death. Hector knew him and had worked with Magnus on the fund raising for the reconstruction after the bombing. Hector was in the drama department and had arranged a series of galas and theatrical events as fund raisers.

"It was funny, I saw Magus with one of my former students just before he died. Magnus was a good man and I had thought he was a good judge of character. When I saw him with Temple Carrier, I almost called him up to warn him off. Temple was a user if there ever was one.

"He was an actor?" John asked.

"He is a bullshit artist and master manipulator," Hector said. "Very experienced, he fooled me for a while and I've spent a life dealing with actors. He was willing to do anything to get a good grade, except do the required work."

"Do you know Wilton Manley?" I asked.

"You've been doing some bottom feeding! I sure do know that snake," Hector said. "He's a classic con artist, but a lot more suave than Temple. He's from a "good family". He's an only child I think. He's one of those guys who think he has to wake up to give the Sun permission to rise. He was in the undergraduate program and I am in charge of the Graduate students, so I wasn't directly associated with him. He had a knack for leading the weak willed astray."

"Are Wilton and Temple friends?" I asked.

"No, not to my knowledge, but they are naturals. Both had an aversion to doing work. Why are you interested?" Hector asked. "Do you think they are involved in Magnus' death?"

"There is something rotten in Denmark. Do you think they are capable of being involved in something like that?" I asked.

"Not murder, at least I don't think Wilton would go that far. We had a student kill himself and the word among the other students was Wilton was involved. He left the department, because there were some who directly blamed him for Tony's death," Hector said. "I wasn't personally involved, but several students I trust were convinced."

"Can you tell me what happened?" I asked.

"As I understand it, Tony DeMelo was a good looking kid from westernmost Virginia, Grundy or Bristol, I think. He had been the star in High School productions and came here with dreams of stardom. He was pretty, whether he was pretty enough, I'm not sure. He had some talent. I saw him in a few productions and he did well."

"Tony also discovered he was gay and he fell under Wilton's spell. Wilton was handsome, worldly and sophisticated to a kid from rural Virginia. Wilton was a few years older and Tony fell for him hook, line and sinker. Unfortunately, Tony wasn't a fool and after a few months of true love, he discovered the true Wilton and cooled it. Well, Wilton had been through a series of boyfriends, but he had always been the dumper, not the dumpee. He took it badly. He took every opportunity to humiliate and embarrass Tony. Wilton always had a group of followers and they piled on the kid."

"Nasty business," John said.

"The big problem came later. Someone sent an anonymous letter to Tony's parents, exposing him as a fag and going into great detail about the boy's sexual tastes," Hector continued. "They showed up at school and there was a nasty scene. Tony jumped off the roof of the Theater Building that night."

"Wilton did it, you think?" I asked.

"I don't think at all, but one of my students was Tony's good friend and roommate. The Parents had left the letter at their apartment when they stormed out. Bruce, that was the roommate, said the information about Tony's sex life was detailed and accurate. Bruce said he was sure Tony had only been with Wilton or him. He sure hadn't sent the letter," Hector said. "What bothered Bruce the most wasn't just the letter, but Wilton's attitude. He seemed excited about the suicide, not remorseful at all."

"Wilton is into power and pain?" John asked.

"That's my read. I've never understood sadism, but I strongly suspect that is part of Wilton's sexual make up," Hector concluded. "I'm gay, but I've never thought of myself as deviant, but Wilton is a certified nut case and dangerous."

"What about Temple" I asked.

"I would guess he's a spear carrier and little else," Hector replied. "But, come to think of it, the only time he put in a decent performance was as an executioner in the "Duchess of Malfi". He only had one line, but he hammed it up royally. That was acceptable for a revenge tragedy. Elizabethans loved blood and gore, but he was animated for the only time in his college career." John went off to get some lunch, leaving me with Hector in the living room talking.

"How long have you known John?" I asked.

"Actually we met five or six years ago, but we were at a party a month ago and seemed to hit it off," he said.

"Something about the way you said that suggests to me you did a lot more that hit it off," I said.

"I know you and John have been friends for a long while," Hector observed cautiously. He looked worried.

"Oh, don't worry about that," I said, realizing what he was worried about. "We are good friends, but no ownership is involved. "You're thinking you and John may be more than friends?"

"That's the feeling I have."

"I hope you're right. John's a great guy. I only want the best for him," I said as John entered the room with a plate of sandwiches.

"What have you guys been talking about?" he asked. I think he may have overheard part of the conversation.

"Hector was afraid you were posted with no trespassing signs. I told him that's not the relationship we have," I said.

Part 9

I went back to the office and called Lonnie to see how he was doing. He asked me to come over and meet his friend. "Pretend you are just stopping by," he asked. Lonnie lived near my office, so I wandered over. Lonnie was in a third floor apartment on Monument Avenue. It was well furnished and I guessed Lonnie had dated an interior decorator at some time in the past. It was also hot as hell there, so both men were shirtless.

Johnny, his friend, was a handsome kid who looked like shit. His eyes were sunken in and he looked exhausted. Johnny was pretty in an oddly masculine way. He was thin, toned and elegant, with beautiful clear blue eyes. He was like one of those Art Deco figurines, sort of Rudolph Valentino. Contrasting with his elegant almost effeminate body, he had a pitch-black beard and thick, dark chest hair. A treasure trail disappeared into his jeans. He also had a deep voice.

"No dress code today, Clydesdale. The air conditioning is broken; we'd be naked if we didn't have company," Lonnie said.

"Don't let me get in the way of your comfort," I replied, as I stripped off my shirt. Johnny all but gasped when he saw my hairy body. If I was bigger, they'd call me a "Gorilla", as it was, "Chimpanzee" was the word that jumps to mind. I do recognize the signs of a guy who is really into body hair and Johnny was one of those. Lonnie noticed too. He winked at me.

Johnnie sat next to me while Lonnie and I talked. He couldn't get his eyes off my body. The kid was all but drooling. We talked about the summer in Richmond and I was afraid Johnnie might have a hands-free orgasm as we talked. Lonnie was a merciful guy and he finally put the boy out of his misery.

"Clydesdale, I was just about ready to jump this boy's ass and have some fun when you dropped in. I can't hold back, so if you don't mind we need some space, unless you want to join us." Lonnie said. If that's okay with Johnny, of course." He looked at Johnny. Johnny had the look of a guy whose fantasy wet dream was coming true.

"I'd like it, Lonnie," he said. "It's fine with me." We went to the bedroom and I dropped my pants and stripped off my jockeys. I caught a brief glimpse of Johnny's cock in his pitch-black bush, but before I could focus, Johnny had my cock in his mouth. My donkey dong had worked its magic again. He took the whole thing while I was still soft. His efforts to swallow felt great, but as soon as I began to get hard, Johnny had to give it up. He had my cock head alone in his mouth by the time I was fully hard.

Johnny was nursing my cock head and fluffing my chest hair, when Lonnie rear-ended him. Lonnie's not my type, but he has nice meat and Johnny liked it.

"Your friend here is nice and friendly, Lonnie," I said. "He's a bit young for me, but he sure took your cock like a pro."

"Johnny's a real nice boy," Lonnie replied. "He's got a nice ass, tight and juicy. He was born to be fucked. You like to fuck, don't you?"

"I sure do, but not with young guys. I like men who have some experience and know how to take a big one," I said. "The last time I fucked a kid, he was more interested in keeping his hair straight than getting down and dirty." I figured if I pretended to be reluctant, it would make Johnny want my cock more. I figured right.

Johnny had already fallen in love with my cock head. I was ready to introduce my head to his prostate. I looked at Lonnie and he could read my mind.

"I bet he can take it," Lonnie said. "I've been giving him lessons in man sex and he has passed every test with flying colors. He opens up wide, and then clamps down when you're in." Lonnie alternated between long deep strokes that probed the deep recesses of Johnny's ass and short pumping movements. The deep strokes almost winded the boy, but he never lost his interest in my cock. He was like a hungry baby who had rediscovered his mother's breast.

"Were you the first to crack his nut?" I asked.

"No, but I was the first to show him what real man sex is like," Lonnie said. "He took my cock like a man and I fucked him every way I could figure. Clydesdale, you know I'm not exactly a virgin; I've got a lot of tricks up my sleeve. The boy's a real pig. He couldn't get enough of my cock. I think I dropped four loads in his ass. It was oozing out the last time I popped him. I scooped some up with my finger and fed it to him. He licked it up."

"Are you ready for big meat, Johnny?" I asked. I held his head in my hands and forced him to stop sucking my cock. "If you want me to fuck you, you'll have to stop sucking." Johnny looked at me. He wanted my cock bad.

"I want it," Johnny croaked.

"Do you mind my cum in his love tunnel?" Lonnie asked.

"The best lube there is. Shoot away!" I said. Lonnie made three or four deep strokes and he shot off. Lonnie moaned as Lonnie rear loaded him. He slowly pulled his cock out. As his cock popped out of Johnny's hole, he ejaculated again and coated the hole with his cum.

"Get on your back," I told Johnny. "I want to see how you're doing." Johnny did as he was told. He was handsome. His skin was pale and contrasted with the silky, black hair on his chest and pubic bush. His tits were bright pink, as was his cock. He was uncut, but since he was rock hard, the skin was pulled back, exposing his purple-blue cock head.

His cock was slightly above average in size and his wide piss slit glistened with precum. He had apricot sized balls, low hangers enclosed in a hairy ball sack.

I hoisted his legs onto my shoulders and positioned my cock at his hole. "Are you ready?" I asked. He nodded. His eyes showed both excitement and fear. He didn't know if he could take it, but he sure wanted to try. I had lubricated my cock, but Lonnie's cum was the only lubricant on Johnny's hole. I pushed.

He resisted for a second or two, and then surrendered. Suddenly my bush was tickling Johnny's balls. He gasped; his cock twitched. A single shot of cum sprayed across Johnny's chest. I have to admit, that turned me on. It was nice to see he had an orgasm on my first stroke. I slowly pulled out and then went in deep again. His ass was tight, but after a few strokes, he was moaning in pleasure. Johnny looked out of it. It was pure, unthinking, sex. Every movement of my cock was matched by Johnny's moans, twitches or spasms.

After his first ejaculation, he was able to hold off for almost ten minutes before he released all of his ball juice. His ass contracted with each ejaculation; I felt as if his ass was milking my cock. This pushed me over the edge.

Johnny had one of those orgasms that are so massive he'd lose weight. I had never seen so much cum. I'm afraid whatever cum he lost, I replaced in the deepest recesses of his rectum. My climax was top of the line. Johnny had almost passed out. The glistening globs of cum that covered Johnny's chest and gut inspired Lonnie. He started licking it up. I just stood there with my cock still ejaculating in his ass.

I began pulling out. Lonnie had started licking his way from Johnny's chest toward the navel. He skipped the gut and extended his tongue and licked the seed still drooling from Johnny's cock head. I had almost pulled out. Only my cock head was still held by the sphincter. It was too good for me to stop, so I shoved my cock back. I ejaculated a last time.

My final thrust had the same effect on Johnny. I would have sworn on a stack of Bibles there wasn't a drop of cum left in the boy's balls. I was wrong. A huge glob sprayed from his cock and landed on Lonnie's tongue. Lonnie loved this.

I pulled out and got on the bed beside Johnny. "You did well kid," I said.

"Shit, I don't believe that happened," Johnny said. Lonnie was more of a sperm hound than I had suspected. Now, he was at the boy's ass, licking up the juices dribbling from Johnny's ass. "Is it like that every time you fuck a guy?" Johnny asked.

"No. It was more intense than usual. We really connected, at least genitally," I said.

"Lonnie said you are a detective. I'm in big time trouble. He said, maybe you could help me," Johnny said.

"Tell me about it."

"I was an investment advisor for a company here in town. It was a good job, the best I ever had," he said.

"What's wrong with that?" I asked, playing stupid.

"If that was it, it would have been fine," Johnny continued. "We specialized in serving rich, older men. Wilton, he's the President, selected prospects. I was to get close to them. I kind of like older men, older than even you, Clydesdale. Wilton told me, the guys were sex starved and if I helped them out, it would make it easier to sell. At first I thought that was sort of a joke."

"My first client was a real nice guy. I liked him a lot and he liked me. We ended up in bed and it was good for both of us. I made a lot on money on that sale. The second client was nice too. The third was a jerk and an ugly jerk at that. I didn't want to have sex with him, but Wilton told me I had too. I could be arrested for doing what I had done. Until that second, I hadn't put two and two together. "

"Upper class call boy?" I said.

"Fucking whore!" Johnny exclaimed. "But it gets worse. I thought it was an investment company. I met a stockbroker at a party. We got friendly and we talked afterward. I mentioned we had most of our investments with his company. He asked me for the name of the company. I told him and he said he had never heard of us. I must have mistaken the name for another broker. I had signed documents from his firm. I told him the names of the guys on the letters. He said the guys either didn't work there, or had been fired years ago. A week later I was at one of Wilton's parties and I discovered the brokerage firm's stationary in a closet. Wilton was making it all up."

"I realize then, the whole company was a fraud. The crooked part wasn't the sex for investment. There were no investments. I didn't know what to do, but that was when one of our clients died. He was Temple's client and Temple had been complaining what a pain he was. Temple was Wilton's right hand man. I think there was something wrong with the whole thing."

"Something worse than prostitution, fraud and embezzlement?" I asked.

"Yes. I am pretty sure blackmail is involved, and maybe..."

"Murder?" I added.

"That's what I am afraid of," Johnny said. "I believe Wilton thinks I know something. He was acting really odd to me the last time we were together."

"Nasty? Rude?"

"No, he was really pleasant, almost fawning. Saying things like, "You're my best boy," sort of stuff."

"You're in a mess," I said. We were silent for a while. "I think this may be a good time for you to disappear. Richmond might not be a good place for you to be right now."

"You know you can stay here," Lonnie said.

"Too close," I said. "Do any of them know you are seeing Lonnie?"

"No," Johnny said. There was another silence. "Oh shit, one guy knows. Temple."

"Bad choice!" I said. "Why don't you come to my house tonight, I will find a place for you." He didn't have any clothes with him. Lonnie said, he would get him some stuff, but it would be better to have no trail.

Johnny and I left and walked back to my office. On the way, I saw John outside his house saying good bye to Hector Bullock. We stopped and talked. Johnny had told me he liked older men and I took a good two or three seconds to realize John and Hector were just what he liked.

Hector was talking about his farm in the country. He was restoring it as a retirement home. He said he was looking for a caretaker to live there to keep an eye on it. Johnny jumped at the opportunity. Hector liked what he saw in Johnny and they hit it off. Hector said they were going to visit the place that evening and Johnny was free to come along and see the place. Everyone was happy about the arrangement, so I returned to the office alone.

I spent the night in my apartment over the office. John called and said they were spending the night at the farm. That was just fine with me. John didn't say it but I had the impression the three of them were hitting it off big time. I got a call from John the next morning.

"We got the whole story from Johnny," he said. "I thought it wasn't believable, but Hector said it's true. He teaches and says it's typical. Most of his students were an odd combination of sophistication and cluelessness. Many of his students hope there is a cushy and easy way to big bucks, with no work and no effort. It's typical; stupid, but typical. And by the way, do you know the kid is the 'Energizer Bunny' of gay sex?" I laughed.

"To tell you the truth, I did have some suspicions," I answered. "He does seem to be open to all the possibilities."

"He's good. Hector has a cock deserving mention in Ripley's Believe It or Not. Johnny took it like a pro. He seemed to get really talkative after sex," John observed.

"I noticed that," I said. It was John's turn to laugh.

"I don't believe I know you so well," John said. "I'm coming home, but Hector's staying here to straighten him out."

"He likes to help young men?"

"He does. Genuinely, he does," John said seriously. "He is a real teacher."

"You like him a lot, don't you?" I asked.

"I do. We share the same interests and like the same things. He's nice to have around the house." John replied. "I was afraid he wanted something different. I've been married and that wasn't so good. I want a friend to grow old with. Someone to depend on, if things turn bad. I didn't want to give up the friends I have and the good times we have. He's great in bed, but having a third in the bed wasn't a problem at all. I was relieved. I wasn't jealous seeing his cock deep into that boy's ass; it turned me on."

"He liked it too?"

"If an orgasm is any indication, he did. He dropped a second load when I shot off in Johnny's ass," John said. "The kid's in danger, isn't he?"

"Yes, I think so," I replied, "just keep him hidden."

Part 10

I went back to the Club to resume my duties in the showers. When I got in, I had a message to call Raleigh. I had left my cell phone in the car and when I went out to get it, Raleigh ran up. He must have been watching for my return.

"Do you have some free time?" he asked. "Jefferson and CW are coming over in ten minutes," I said, "Yes; I'm not on duty until three. Play session?"

"I need to talk," Raleigh said. "And, come to think of it, some play might be welcome too!" He smiled. "Do you think we could do both?"

"I know we can!" I replied. "I'll see you in a few minutes." I retrieved my phone, dropped my stuff in my room and went to the Governor's cottage. Jefferson was already there. The Governor was away for the day at a grandchild's birthday party.

"Glad you could get over here so quickly. Poor Jefferson needs some cock," Raleigh said.

"Why didn't you take care of him? You didn't need to wait," I said.

"Jefferson here likes white meat," Raleigh replied. "My black man-rammer doesn't ring his chimes anymore."

"I know of white guys who like black cock, but I didn't know black guys had the same interest," I said. We were all moving toward the bedroom and were stripping as we walked. "Is a redneck cock by any chance, better than plain old white guy meat?" I asked. Jefferson laughed.

"I'm not sure, but I have a suspicion that might be true," Jefferson said. "I'd sure like to find out though." We were all naked by now. We got on the bed. I sucked Raleigh while Jefferson sucked me. I liked being in the middle and Jefferson was genuinely enthusiastic about my cock. After a few minutes, we got down to heavy duty fucking.

People talk about tight buns, but Jefferson had an ass more like a bear trap. He had no problem taking CW's cock a week earlier. My cock was different. I had to force it in. I'm not into force, but Jefferson was. He was both fighting me and telling me to fuck him hard and force it in. He wanted a pretend rape. He wanted to be forced to take my cock. I had fucked him before, but he had an ability to turn virgin between fuck sessions. His ass was just as tight as the first time.

I added more lube to my cock and went at him again. I finally popped through his sphincter and rammed him to the hilt in a single thrust. Jefferson sighed in deep satisfaction. There was no doubt I hit all the right spots. I was still for a few seconds, and then began pumping slowly. As I stroked, Jefferson began to shiver every time my cock went as deep as it could go.

I hadn't been sure how much Jefferson was role-playing and how much was real. The shivering was real. I knew that and Raleigh noticed it too.

"Damn, you got him going!" Raleigh said. "I've only seen that happen once before. Hot!" CW entered the bedroom and joined us. It was hard to believe a guy could strip as fast as he did. He was fully dressed and seconds later he was naked and hard. Jefferson was moaning non-stop by now.

"Damn, that looks good. Raleigh, would you mind taking me for a ride?" CW asked. "It's been a while since I've had real meat up my ass."

"Why, that's the best offer I've had today," Raleigh said. "I do want to watch Jeffy pop. Can you flop him over and screw him spread eagled? That will give us a good view of the fireworks." I pulled out and got Jefferson on his back. His cock was so hard it looked as if it hurt. I put his legs on my shoulders.

Just as I did that, our eyes met. He had a desperate look. He wanted my cock in his ass. I shoved my cock hard. He tried to resist, but couldn't keep my pole out. His eyes rolled back in his head and he had a look of total satisfaction on his face. With every stroke of my cock, a glob of precum oozed from his bloated cock.

C. W. climbed on the bed and got on his hands and knees.

"Straddle Jefferson," Raleigh instructed. "That will give you a front row seat." C. W. did what he was told. As soon as he was in position, Raleigh was on the bed and thrust his cock deep into CW's innards.

"Holy Shit!" CW exclaimed.

"Is it too much?" Raleigh asked.

"No," whispered CW The young man wiggled his ass, and then ground it in a circular movement. I like to watch a master bottom accommodate himself to a cock. Soon CW was undulating his ass, rubbing Raleigh's cock against his prostate. CW was on his hands and knees over Jefferson. He dropped down so his mouth was inches away from Jefferson's rock hard dick. That opened his ass a bit more so if Raleigh had another inch of meat, he could get it in the love canal. CW liked it a lot and could take anything Raleigh could force in.

CW had a front row seat to watch my cock pound the black man's ass.

"Ain't this just the scene for the NAACP to promote racial harmony?" Raleigh observed. CW and Jefferson were 69ing while each was impaled of the cock of a man of the other race. "There are no black or white cocks, only hard cocks!"

"That seems to be true, but it's going to be hard to turn that into a public service ad on television," I said. "A hard cock is a terrible thing to waste."

"Shit!" CW exclaimed. "I'm close!" He was shooting cum across Jefferson's smooth body. The spurting warm sperm pushed Jefferson over the edge. Jefferson's ass contracted with each ejaculation. It felt great. I rested and let him catch his breath, then pulled out slowly. His ass was still so tight it held my foreskin in place while I pulled my shaft out. I was far more relaxed than I had thought. My cock was out of his ass, but his hole still held the tip of my foreskin.

Raleigh was out too. He hadn't shot off either. Both CW and Jefferson looked wasted.

"You boys look tired, but I'm going to need someone to take my load sometime this morning," Raleigh said

"If you don't mind waiting 20 minutes, I'd be glad to help you out," C. W. said.

"I can help too. How in hell did you old guys keep from shooting," Jefferson cried. "That was one fucking hot scene."

"I just keep my powder dry," I said. "I almost shot off when I deep dicked you, but I held back. Once I've done that, it takes a lot of work to pop the balloon."

"I'm preoccupied by other things," Raleigh replied. "I'm worried about the Governor. Some thing's not right."

"You mean that asshole is finally treating you like a human being?" Jefferson asked. Raleigh laughed.

"Not that, I'm afraid. His little sex-buddy-son-substitute wants to take him away for a weekend," Raleigh said. That little snake Jason described it as, "A weekend with the boys!" It bothers me. Something is up and it isn't good."

"The Governor and his wallet are both invited, I would bet!" I said.

"I'm not as worried about the wallet as the will," Raleigh said.

"The will?" CW asked.

"Yes. It's to be a planning retreat for financial and estate advice," Raleigh answered."I have tried to explain it to the Governor's daughter, but she doesn't think it's a problem."

"No way I'd let him go," I said. "I think Jason is dangerous."

"You do?" CW said. "Are you serious?"

"I'm afraid I am," I said emphatically, "dead serious." There was silence.

"Why do you think that?" Raleigh asked. "Are you what you say you are? Somehow you know a lot more than a towel boy should." I know I should have kept my cover, but I figured Governor Johnson was in physical danger, so I leveled with them and explained the situation. There looked shocked, but with the personalities of the men involved, there was no problem believing it.

"Well, that explains a lot," said Raleigh. "Things didn't seem right, but I didn't guess the situation was that serious."

CW observed, "Wilton and his boys are not like the other guys here. I thought they were just working boys after an easy screw and a free dinner. It's funny; I'm willing to jump into bed with just about any guy who asked. No one does." He paused. "Well, almost no one does. I'm happy draining their balls and am more than willing to leave their bank accounts untouched. I have to admit I'm a bit worried about the judgment of conservative Republicans. I knew their political ideas were off base. How can they be that bad a judge of character? I may not be as cute, but I'm better hung and great in bed."

The phone rang. It was a State Trooper. The Governor had been in an accident and was on his way to the University Hospital in Charlottesville. His car had gone off the road and into a tree. Quite frankly, the idea that the governor was driving at all scared me shitless. Our party was over. I went back to my room and got ready for work. I got on the bed for a quick nap and there was a knock on my door. It was Donovan.

"What's your game, Clydesdale? I know who you are. Who are you investigating?" he asked.

"Not you," I replied. He looked relieved. "I'm checking out Wilton and his sidekicks."

"What's their game then?"

"It looks like he's into fraud, embezzlement, blackmail," I said, "and prostitution. There may be some worse crimes involved, too. It's an evolving situation. They prey on wealthy, conservative men. After they take their money, they figure the threat of exposure of being gay will give them immunity from prosecution. It's a neat scheme."

"Fucking shit! I'm screwed!" he cried. "We're all screwed. If this gets out... a lot of guys are ruined."

"I'm after the bad guys, not the victims," I said. "I don't want to ruin anyone if I can possibly avoid it. There may be some narrow-minded hypocrites here, but that ain't a crime. It may be a sin and it's sure unattractive, but not a crime. I've never outed anyone in my life and I'm not going to start now. Even if they deserve it, I just can't do it." He looked at me closely. I looked him square in the eye.

"I deserve it. I know that," Donovan said.

"You're not telling me anything I don't know," I said smiling. "I'm at peace with myself; I know what I am and what I like. Being gay carries a lot of baggage with it, too much for some guys. Maybe it's too much most guys. If you can't deal with it, it's too bad, but that's none of my business."

"Is there any way out of this?" Donovan asked.

"I had thought maybe we could leave it as it is. Wilton's marks can afford the loss, but one of his victims killed himself and another met with an "accident". I need to stop him, but I don't know how yet. He's after Governor Johnson now."

"I noticed," Donovan said. "It makes my skin crawl." He was silent for a while. "Are you opposed to punishment without a trial?"

"As a matter of fact, no," I said. "When I was a cop, I use to administer some corporal punishment at the moment of apprehension. I did it only when the perp was caught in the act, though. The deaths in this case make it difficult. I've turned one of his boys. He told me the entire plan. I could take it to the police and get then all put away, but it seems the cost would be too high for the victims."

"Maybe Wilton or Jason will find the wrong person. Some guys aren't too forgiving of this sort of thing," Donovan said.

"I don't exactly know what that means," I said, "and I'm not going to ask either," Donovan looked at me again and smiled.

"I don't know why, but I trust you," he said.

"Let me ask you a favor of you. You might just see who's been hooked and either let me know, or warn them away," I said. "Do it carefully, so we don't scare them off, but you might let some guys know about your unease."

"I can do that," he said. He turned to leave and then turned back. "I am off to Washington for the rest of the day. Are you going to be here tomorrow night?"

"Sure. I'm here every night, ready, willing and able," I said.

"I wasn't thinking about that," he said.

"Donovan. I told you I am at ease with myself. I have no problem admitting I like what I like," I said. "Relax. It's fine with me, whatever you want." He left.

The afternoon at the heath club was busier than usual. It was a rainy day and many of the men decided to exercise at the club rather than golf. There was a younger group there. It was made up of congressional aides who were here for a seminar. The presenter for the afternoon session failed to show, so they had the afternoon off.

These men were pale and rather pasty looking. These were the guys who did the real work for the Congressmen and they clearly didn't get out the office much. Most of the men were driven, over achievers and weren't too sensible about reasonable amounts of exercise. There were going to be a lot of sore muscles the next morning.

They weren't very pleasant either. Most thought I was a personal servant. It was odd to be with people who only barked orders and made no effort to be civil. These were people who were use to being rude to waitresses. They all went off to dinner and an evening seminar and I got a much needed break.

One guy was left. He had arrived later than the others and was even paler than them. I'm not sure he had ever seen the sun. He was maybe in his early 30s and would be in bad shape by the time he was 40. He had dark hair and was attired in new exercise clothes, which had clearly never been worn before. I showed him how to use the machines and went to clean up the shower and steam room.

Someone had been playing with the hose and I soaked myself when I hosed down the area. It had been set to spray. When I was done, it was approaching closing time. I checked up on him. He had been working out for a good hour and a half. He was puffing away on a leg lift machine.

"Take it easy, you'll hurt yourself," I said. "Don't strain yourself."

"It says you're supposed to do thirty reps," he said.

"You work up to that, you don't start there," I explained. "You can stop now." He looked relieved.

"Are you sure?"

"Hey, pal, I work here. Do what you are comfortable with. Don't overdo it," I said.

"I don't exercise much," he said. "The guys were telling me I need to work out more."

"Few guys here do it regularly," I told him.

"They sure talk as if they do," he said. "I felt like the kid with sand being kicked in his face by the bullies at the beach."

"Bullshit! It's all talk," I told him. "They talk the talk, but don't walk the walk." He got up and moaned.

"I'm stiff already," he complained.

"A hot shower and long steam will solve that problem," I said as I pointed the way to the showers. He wandered off.

A few minutes later the shower was going. I looked in. The man turned away from me when he saw me and slipped on the soapy floor. I was close enough to grab him and keep him from hitting the floor.

"Careful there, Buddy, it's slippery here." As I said that, I saw he had an erection. He was smooth and pink, with femininely delicate looking skin. He had a long, thick cock and bull balls. When he saw I noticed his hard-on, he turned bright red.

"Nice equipment you have there, pal," I added. "The other guys may have some muscle, but you've got the muscle that counts." He relaxed.

"You think so?" he asked. It's always a safe bet to compliment a guy on the size of his equipment. In this case it was true and the guy blushed in pleasure. "My name is Edwin."

"Will, here. I know so. I work here. I see a lot of cock, and I know cock forwards and backwards!" Then, I cupped his balls. "You got the baby factory and the delivery system," He laughed. "Try out the stream room. You'll need to loosen up."

I went back to my work. Edwin went into the steam room. About ten minutes later I checked on him again. The room was solid steam and I couldn't see at all.

"Are you in there Edwin?"

"Yes, here in the back," he said. "Come and join me." I had closed the Health Club, so I was off duty.

"I'm not supposed to use the facilities here, but if you won't tell, I'd be glad to loosen up."

"I promise," he said, "Scouts' Honor." The way he said it made me think he was serious. There was something about him that suggested Eagle Scout. I took off my shirt and shorts and went back into the steam.

"Damn, you're a hairy one!" said Edwin as I got near enough for him to see. He wasn't hard, but he wasn't soft either. "And hung too!"

"Aw, shucks. We all have the cards God gave us," I said as I sat next to him. He was staring at my cock and his cock was rising. Edwin turned red again as he realized what was happening. "I don't want to sound tacky, Edwin, but I do appreciate you giving me a show," I said. "There's something about a big cock that seems to hit the spot."

"You're not grossed out?"

"Shit no."

"I've always been embarrassed by it. The kids made fun of me at school," Edwin said. He sounded like a little boy who had done something wrong, but didn't know exactly what it was. "Father Kelly told me it was dirty to think about it, or touch it."

"Edwin, you've been hanging out with the wrong crowd," I said. Reaching over I stroked his cock a few times. It twitched and a shot of cum spurted out.

"Oh God!" he cried. "I've never done that before!"

"Nice show," I said. "It's nice to be appreciated. Do you ever taste your own cum?" He shook his head. "Do you mind if I try it?" He nodded. I collected some of his spunk on my finger and ate it. When I pulled the finger out of my mouth I collected the rest of the milky fluid on the same finger.

"What does it taste like?" he asked in whisper.

"Well, it's never going to replace M&M's as a taste treat, but it's the basis of all human life on earth. Every man's is different and individual. It turns me on when a guy offers it to me." Edwin opened his mouth and I stuck my finger into it. He sucked it like a starved baby.

"Okay?" I asked. He nodded. "Now let me tell you something. You can walk away right now and the night is over. We both will have had a little bit of fun. If you stay, I'm going to get every drop of your man spunk out to your balls and into my throat." My cock was well on its way to a full erection. Edwin reached over and stroked it. Pulling the skin back, exposing my cock head. A big glob of precum emerged from my slit.

"Is that your cum?" he asked. Edwin was away from home and no one was watching. He was ready to take a big leap.

Part II

Edwin wasn't really my type and I'm not sure Edwin knew enough about man-sex to have a type, but we had a good time anyway. I had the strange feeling I was introducing him to his cock and all of its potential for the first time. He was virgin and innocent.

Edwin was one of those rare guys who believed all the old wives tales about masturbation. The Priest had told him not to do it and he didn't. More correctly, he didn't do it often. He had been guilt ridden about his failures in that area. Every time he shot off, he was consumed with guilt. I was the first man, or woman for that matter, to touch his cock. Guilt isn't my thing and I told him it was stupid. I gave a brief explanation about the subject and pointed out a mere 99% of men did it. He believed me and thirty years of pent-up sexual desires and needs came to the surface.

It's funny, but I would bet his Priest thought he was saving Edwin from sin and degradation. In fact his was condemning him to a joyless existence. I never understood why God would make us complete with an easily accessible organ capable of generating the greatest physical pleasure a man can experience, and then say using it was a sin. That's not rational. While jerking off is good, it pales in comparison to sex with a fellow human being. Sex is meant to be shared.

I am no Mother Theresa, but I did my best to straighten him out. I may not have saved him, but he sure was a lot more relaxed when he left than when he came into the exercise room. He didn't know what to do, what was okay and what was off limits. I broadened Edwin's view of what was acceptable by a goodly amount. There was one odd aspect to Edwin's view of sex. He had a sheltered life, living with his mother until a year earlier when she died. He knew fucking a woman was sinful unless you were married, but he had no real conception of sex with a man.

Edwin also knew what felt good. The single ejaculation caused when I stroked his cock was the closest to real sex he had ever been. He also liked the feel of my cock. He had never done that either.

"Stroke until it's hard!" I told him.

"It feels so good," he murmured. "I don't believe it feels so good."

"If you think this is good, boy are you in for a good night," I said, as I leaned over and took his cock head into my mouth. He moaned when my tongue touched it, but he didn't shoot off right away. I had been afraid of that. Edwin was oozing precum and enjoying every moment. After a minute or two, I came up for breath.

"Thank you, that was great," Edwin whispered. "Do I have to do that to you?" he added, with uncertainty in his voice. I felt sorry for him. He didn't know the rules and was afraid he would do something wrong. I smiled at him.

"Nope, it's not required," I said. "Not if you don't want to."

"How do you know if you want to?"

"I'm afraid you're the only one who can answer that," I said. Edwin looked me in the eyes.

"You wouldn't mind if I tried it, would you?" I didn't need to answer that question. Edwin approached my cock very gingerly, but once his tongue touched it he was hooked. You could say he was a slow started, but a fast learner. Once he started, he didn't want to stop. I finally pulled him off.

"You know what's going to happen if you don't slow down?" I asked. Edwin looked puzzled. "You're going to end up with a mouth full of my man seed!" I explained.

"Is that bad?" he asked.

"Not for me, but I was worried you'd be shocked when I shot my load down your throat."

"Would you take mine?" he asked.

"Sure, but I've got a lot more experience. I don't want to you to go too far and be uncomfortable."

"I think I want to try it," Edwin said, slowly. "Am I being dumb about this? I've never done anything like this before. And I do mean anything!"

"Let's get out of this steam room and go to my bedroom," I suggested. "It's more comfortable and private there." We left the room, showered and went to my bedroom, which is next to the locker area.

"What do we do now?" Edwin asked.

"Why don't we take off the towels and see what happens?"

"I was hoping you would say something like at," Edwin said, smiling. He dropped his towel. "For years I told myself real pleasure was spiritual, not physical. Do you think that's true, or just a crock?"

"I don't think there is anything wrong with either. I think sexual pleasure's pretty good alone or with a good dose of spiritual pleasure," I said. "I admit it doesn't always happen, but it's real good when it does. Sometimes you really connect."

"Like when you get married?" he asked.

"I've never been married, so I don't know. But there's nothing wrong with two guys enjoying themselves," I said. "You're adult; I'm adult. I'm not tricking you into sex, am I?" Edwin laughed.

"I'm ruined!" he cried in mock horror. "I've lost my virginity! I was saving myself for the wedding night!" He paused. "You know, I told myself that many times, but I never actually dated a woman."

"You use to watch Tarzan and Hercules movies?" I asked. Edwin looked shocked and then he laughed.

"You've been there?"

"Sure," I said, stroking his cock. "We all have. Too much talk and not enough play, let's get at it again."

On the bed in my room I discovered several interesting things about Edwin. He had a throat like one of those snakes that can swallow animals three times their size. We tried 69ing and from that angle, Edwin could take my entire cock. Not only could he take it, he was comfortable taking it. My cock got more quality time down his throat that night than I normally get in a year.

Since he had so little idea what man sex was like, I also introduced him to his anal Adventure Land. He knew little about the possibilities of his cock; I'm not sure he knew his prostate existed.

I discovered his magic nut was the length of my index finger up his ass. I reached it quickly and pressed it hard. It is possible he would have complained about me shoving a finger up his ass, but he was moaning in ecstasy before he had a chance. Like his cock and balls, Edwin's prostate was over sized and overripe.

I got him to sit up against the headboard, with his legs spread and raised. I worked two fingers in to his ass while I sucked his cock. He was all but crying as I squeezed the juice out of his prostate and sucked it from his cock. He was a happy guy. I was a happy guy too. I had done a good deed and had a good time to boot.

Edwin went back to his room at about midnight. He was short two or three generous loads of cum. Before he left, I shot a full load of my spunk down his gullet while he was deep throating me. I'm not sure he even tasted it, my cock was so deep. He did know I was climaxing. I had a five-alarm orgasm. It was hard to believe I didn't shoot a major internal organ down his throat. The ejaculations were that strong.

The next day was quiet in the morning and became progressively less quiet and even productive as the day progressed. Governor Johnson was out of the hospital and Raleigh brought him back to the cottage. Raleigh enforced a strict, "No Visitors" policy and kept the old man away from the sharks. Donovan returned with Charley, Hal and Henry in tow. They were golfing all day.

I called the office in Richmond and Lance reported all was well. Apparently the action had shifted from Richmond, toward the Club and Washington. Wilton had set his sights on bigger fish. That made sense to me. Richmond is a comparatively small city and Washington presented more appealing and far wealthier targets.

I called John and he had some more information. The rumor mill was in overdrive and the word was out that all was not right with Magnus' accident. Johnny and Hector Bullock were hitting it off well and Hector's campaign to reform the boy was well under way.

"Hector says, the boy is a first class size queen and Hector was using his natural assets to make the boy see the light," John reported. "According to Hector, ten inches of cock up his ass makes Johnny very receptive to reason!"

"Shit, ten inches makes even me reasonable!" I said. John laughed.

"Come to think of it, it has the same effect on me!" John added.

The golfers were out on the course, so the exercise room was all but empty until Wilton arrived with all of his minions. Jason and Temple were there as well as two other guys I didn't recognize. I sure did know the type. I wanted to get near them to listen in on the conversation, but they hushed up when I came in range. CW and Jefferson came in to exercise. CW was management and Jefferson was his guest, so they got in. I mentioned to CW and Jefferson I wanted to get near Wilton.

"No problem," Jefferson said. "We have a connection with those guys." He leaned near me and whispered, "Cocks are the universal language. Wilton likes to look at dark meat. He's never sampled it yet, but he sure is interested."

"Watch your step," I said.

"Sure," Jefferson said, "I do need to watch for drool. I might slip on it!" They went off. Jefferson exercised shirtless and wore lightweight polyester shorts with no jock underneath. Nothing was left to the imagination. He was muscular and shaved his body, so he looked like a sculpture. He went over next to Wilton and started exercising.

I glanced over at them and it was clear Wilton liked what he saw. Nothing is more desirable than forbidden fruit and Jefferson was forbidden fruit. Wilton and several of his boys were talking to themselves and taking quick glances at Jefferson. They wandered off to the shower and steam room.

CW was babbling to Temple. CW could play the idiot convincingly. He defined brainless and he also was an easy lay. Temple had had to work to get Magnus. I knew from my chats with Magnus, Temple had bottomed for the older man. Temple wanted some top time and he wanted it in a younger, firmer ass. CW met the bill. They went to the steam room too.

Wilton emerged a half hour later from the stream room. He with his friends dressed and left. Jefferson had to leave to wait tables, but C.W came over to me and told what they had learned. Wilton apparently had the instincts of a wild animal. He knew something was amiss and no longer felt comfortable in Richmond. Wilton was planning to move his base north to Washington. He was also thinking about an island retreat. That confirmed Lance's report.

Jason mentioned an inheritance. CW didn't know who it was from, but I did. I would tell Raleigh to keep the Governor firmly buttoned up. Temple was seeing a man named Rudy. I didn't know who he was, but CW said he was a retired banker from Chicago who was at the Club for a month or two. CW noticed a sharp exchange between Temple and Wilton.

"Apparently Temple went too far with something in Richmond. He got "carried away" and Wilton didn't like it at all," CW said. "Temple didn't admit anything, but he said it wouldn't happen again. Then he switched the conversation to Rudy. Rudy is a fat cat with money to spare."

"What is Rudy like?"

"Not exactly a stud muffin, if you get my drift. His wife is on a two month trip to Europe with his grandchildren. He's not in very good health and doesn't seem well equipped to live alone. They have servants, but he apparently is pretty much helpless without his wife, or at least she doesn't want the house routine disrupted while she is gone. He's here until they get back," CW explained.

"I haven't seen him here," I said.

"He's fat and ugly. Moving isn't his thing. He's been a problem for the housekeeping staff. He can't bend over to pick up things from the floor. The room is always a mess," CW continued. "His only exercise is to get from his room to the dining room twice a day. He can play cards too, but that's about it. Jefferson was nearer and got the whole conversation. He'll get in touch with you after work."

"Thanks for the report. You've been a help," I said. As CW left, Henry came in.

"Donovan told what was up here," he said. "This is an awful mess."

"Shit, I don't want everyone and his brother getting in on this!" I said.

"Clydesdale, there aren't any guys more interested in keeping this quiet than us. If this gets out there are scores of men whose careers and families will be ruined," Henry said. "Mine included."

"I don't kiss and tell. Your secret is safe with me."

"I know that, but I'm not the problem, my boss has been "investing" with Wilton," Henry said.

"You're shitting me! That pompous, moralizing ass is taking a roll in the hay with Wilton? Senator Baldridge has a taste for twink cock?"

"I don't know about the roll in the hay, but his bank account is lighter by $30,000.00," Henry explained. "I'm afraid that converts into several rolls in the hay. The good Senator has a clueless wife and three nice kids. They'd be hamburger if it got out. "

"I've sometimes thought the biggest assholes get the sweetest wives. It must be some sort of a defense mechanism," I said. "How do you work for a guy like that?"

"I'm afraid it's an unattractive combination of ambition and self delusion. At one time, it seemed to me Baldridge was a right-minded

112

man supporting the values I admire. The Senator was also my ticket out of small town America and into the big leagues," he said. "By the time I realized all his moral stands were part of solidifying his political base and just a front, Washington was too much for me to give up."

"When did you see the light?"

"I saw a glimmer that night in your bedroom. It was pure enjoyment. It wasn't what I thought it would be like at all. Damn your cock turned me on," Henry said. "And Donovan wasn't my idea of a flaming fagot either. When I got back to Washington, the Senator's bookkeeper asked me about Wilton. He had found three unexplained checks, each for $10,000.00. I ran into Donovan. He told me about the scam. I put two and two together and saw the light."

"You ran into Donovan?" I asked. Henry looked sheepish.

"I guess you could say we had a date," he admitted.

"And how was the sex?" Henry blushed.

"Good. I guess you know more about me, than I do."

"You're a man and I'm a man. I'm not completely clueless," I said. "It's okay, you know. Sex is a part of life and it's okay to like it. As a matter of fact, I like it a lot myself." Henry laughed.

"Much to my surprise, I like it a lot too," he admitted. "The sex wasn't as good as with you the other night. I found myself thinking about you."

"Me or my cock?" Henry thought a few seconds.

"I'd guess 40% you and 60% your cock."

"I'll bet it was more like 30% me and 70% my cock!" I said. "Don't worry, there's nothing you can do about it. I don't think there's much you can do about what turns you on. I don't think you have any way to control if you like males or females. Most gay guys seem to like smooth boys; I like hairy men and I like them big and brawny. I can't change that; you can't change your taste in men or in cocks for that matter. Relax and don't worry. You're lucky."

"How's that?"

"Think about the guys so deep in the closet they never act on their desires. They never experience sexual release or satisfaction. They go through life never feeling intense pleasure or passion," I explained.

"They get mean, don't they?" Henry said. "Mean and bitter."

"That seems to be the way it goes. It sure looks that way from my vantage point. Your Senator Baldridge rants and raves at the people who enjoy life and gets a little fun on the sly," I said. "Baldridge is a jerk and an asshole, but he's pathetic too. A pathetic, mean spirited shell, who tried to grab some fun from a con man's prick. I guess there's some poetic justice to that. He attacked that gay Priest last year, who seemed kind and compassionate and ends up in bed with Wilton." A group of men entered the room and our conversation was over. Henry had a lot of thinking to do. I didn't know if he would make the right choice.

In the late afternoon, the exercise room filled to capacity and I was busy. Most were new me, but my reputation as a lifesaver had spread and most were pleasant. Most did what I asked them to do too. When I told them to stop, they obeyed me, so I had no problems. After work I went on a walk and passed by the Governor's cottage. I heard Raleigh emphatically stating, "The Governor's in bed! He was in an accident and he needs his sleep! You white boys have no sense at all!"

The two men, I think it was Jason and another guy, left. I knocked on the door. Raleigh appeared loaded for bear. When he saw me, he looked relieved.

"I can't tell you how tired I am of uppity white boys! Give me a horse-hung, redneck any day!" he exclaimed. "Come on in, you are welcome!"

"How are you doing?" I asked.

"I'm pissed off, but good. I do have reinforcements. Meet my Uncle Joe. He's cooking some, sitting with the Governor and guarding the back door." Uncle Joe was an older, tall man with a bushy white beard encasing a pitch black face. He smiled as we shook hands.

"You needed reinforcements?" I asked.

"I sure did. The accident seems to have discombobulated the Governor. He's completely lost. Got up in the middle of the night and made a cup of coffee. He almost burned the house down. Turned on every burner in the kitchen and forgot to put the water in the pot," Raleigh said.

"I'm sorry. Is it time for him to go to a home?"

"Shit, that man has needed to be in a home since his son died, not that he was ever much good of a man," Uncle Joe interjected. "I was the first black teacher in the local High School. Governor Johnson tried to make a special example of me."

"Joe was the Latin teacher. And winning football coach," Raleigh explained.

"The Latin didn't help at all, but the winning football coach was too much for even the Governor to fight!" Joe said. "Sometimes life isn't fair, but it isn't predictable either. Now, I take it you are the pint sized, cock master Raleigh told me about?"

"Raleigh, just exactly how many horse hung, pygmies do you know?" I asked. Both men burst out laughing.

"He said, you have a sense of humor, I was just checking," Joe said. There was a huge crash in the Governor's bedroom. He had gotten out of bed and had pulled over a dresser. After a quick check it seemed he was fine. He was muttering something about a ladder falling over. Apparently he had been trying to climb the dresser. I helped get him back in bed and went back to the club.

Part 12

Later that night Donovan appeared and tried to pump me for more information on Wilton's scam. It was clear to me he was trying to find out how bad the exposure of conservative Republicans was to the potential scandal. He winced when I mentioned several names. It wasn't a good day for ultra conservative moralists.

"I don't believe I didn't have a fucking clue!" he exclaimed. "I make my living knowing things like this." Before I had a chance to ask him how exactly he made his living, my phone rang. It was CW.

"Get to the pool, pronto!" he said. "Big trouble!" I raced to the pool, which was next to the exercise club with Donovan right behind me. A body floated face down in the water. I arrived as CW came from his office overlooking the pool and Raleigh and Joe emerged from the bushes.

"Oh my God!" Raleigh cried. "Is it the Governor? He escaped!"

It was dark, CW went to turn on the pool lights, but I didn't think it was the Governor. The body didn't look large enough. As soon as the lights came on it was obvious the body wasn't him; it was a much younger man. In my gut I knew it was Jason. I could hear a siren in the distance.

"Are we sure he's dead?" Donovan asked.

"Shit!" I said, realizing we had been just standing around. I jumped in the water and swam to the body. I touched it. "He's dead," I yelled. "He's been dead a while!" I swam under the body and confirmed it was Jason. I went back to the edge of the pool and got out.

Raleigh and Joe were calling for Governor Johnson. Jefferson and several of the staff joined in the search. The pool was on the backside of the club, since many of the members didn't like the noise the pool generated. The Rescue Squad and a County Policeman arrived. I told them the man was dead. The squad wanted to fish him out but the cop, Deputy Willis, thought something was amiss and called in for more backup.

Like a ghost, the bloated figure of the Governor emerged from bushes on the side of the pool. He was soaked, cut and bruised. He staggered towards to edge of the pool, saw the body and cried out "Jimmy!" in a horrified scream. He collapsed. The Rescue Squad rushed over to his aid.

For a while it seemed as if the Governor had a heart attack. The local rescue vehicles were equipped as emergency cardiac units. They got the elderly man into it and raced off to the UVA Hospital. Raleigh went with them. As he left, two police cruisers drove up. A Deputy got out of one car; a Deputy and plain clothes detective came from the other. The detective was Butch McRoy, the former head guard at the prison I had worked at fifteen years earlier. He had retired a few years before and I'd lost touch with him.

His eyes met mine; I shook my head and he went on as if he didn't recognize me. He introduced himself as Detective Barton McRoy and started to question us. He knew a bad situation when he saw it. Jason was fully dressed in a suit and tie. As I got use to the bright light, I could see there was an obvious bruise on the side of his head. Butch wanted the Medical Examiner to be there when the body was removed from the water. He questioned CW and Joe in detail and went on to question Donovan. When he came to me, he didn't change his approach at all. There was no sign anything was different with me.

I told him it was a guest, Jason, who had died. I had confirmed he was dead, but had done nothing else to disturb the body.

He made a call on his cell phone and then came back to us. "I called Judge Wilson and he has authorized search warrants for the club and all rooms and cottages associated with it," he reported to us. "If there is no objection, I'd like to start the search now." He got Uncle Joe to go with a Deputy to search the Governor's cottage and CW to take another to search Jason's room. He told Donovan and the other on lookers to return to the club and keep any suspicions about the events here quiet.

"You mean there's been an accident in the pool?" Donovan said in an innocent voice. Donovan took a long look at Butch and liked what he saw. The look was not so innocent. "I'll say the local yokels are being officious about an ordinary accident."

"That story sounds good to me," Butch said. He had checked out Donovan as he spoke. Butch liked masculine men; Donovan was his type. Strangely, I suspected he and Donovan had recognized the mutual interest. Maybe there is such a thing as gaydar. Everyone left, leaving Butch and me alone.

"What's up here?" Butch asked. "I've got a nose for crime and this whole set-up stinks to high heavens."

"How does homosexual prostitution, embezzlement, blackmail and maybe murder sound?" I asked. "All of that, by the way, is wrapped in conservative, born-again, America the Beautiful politics."

"Is this the only murder?" Butch asked.

"Probably it's the second; possibly there's a third. There's been one automobile accident and a suicide." I said.

"That philanthropist in Richmond?" Butch asked.

"You've heard about it?"

"My friends in Richmond say there is something wrong with his death. High ranking politicos badly wanted it to be an accident," Butch said. "The City Police wouldn't let it go. There is no satisfactory resolution yet, but the case is still open."

"Magnus was a good man. He deserved better. Did they tell you anything?" I said.

"You're working on the case?" he asked. "They told me to keep my eyes open; one of their suspects was headed my way."

"Yes, I can tell you anything you want, but it's mostly guesswork," I said, "You're looking good. I had no idea you were so near. Where have you been?"

"I went back to North Carolina and took care of mom for few years after retirement. Mom died and I came back to Virginia. Actually the local man here had a heart attack and they needed a substitute. I came and stayed," Butch said. "I've been here about four years. Where can I set up a headquarters here?"

"You're welcome to use the exercise area. It's right next door," I said showing him the side entrance to the club. "Showers, steam room and exercise equipment, with my bedroom next door."

Butch smiled at me. "It's like old times! Do you get lucky often?"

"Every fucking night!" I said. "How's your love life? Have you become a monk yet?"

He smiled. "Let's say I been able to recruit some real nice guys for the force."

I gave him a quick summary of Wilton's scheme and listed the main characters, including Temple, the prime suspect in Magnus' death. Butch took notes. I told him about the Governor and his relationship with Jason. I finished just in time for the Medical Examiner to arrive with the State Police Mobile Crime Lab. I was able to watch.

I told them the approximate location of the Governor's appearance and showed them where he collapsed. I didn't know how he got away from Raleigh and Joe, but he had gotten out somehow. They moved the body at 1:00 a.m. and I got to bed at 2:00 in the morning. I woke at six, went out to the pool area and found Butch had returned with a new crew of men to search the site.

I went over to the Governor's Cottage. Raleigh drove up as I got there. "He's under sedation. It isn't a heart attack. He thinks his son died a second time," Raleigh said. "His daughter is with him now."

"A long night?" I asked. "You need to get to bed."

"What's up here?" he asked. I gave him a rundown. Joe saw us talking in the driveway and came out, filling us in on details. I told them I knew Butch and he was a good man to have on the job.

"He's not going to railroad the Governor?" Joe asked.

"Don't worry about that. He's reasonable," I said. I went back to my room. Butch, Willis and another guy were discussing the case at a table. They all looked bushed. The Deputy I didn't know was covered in mud. One of the EMTs had joined them.

"Clydesdale, you know Willis, the other Deputy is Donnie, and the EMT is Josh. Men, this is Clydesdale. He's an old friend of mine and I'd just as soon not have that known around here," Butch said. "He's undercover."

"Are you the one who caught the bomber?" Josh asked. I nodded. It always surprised me when people knew who I was.

"What happened to the Governor?" Butch asked.

"As far as we could tell, he fell after being beaten up or assaulted," Butch said. The top of his body had been in the pool, the bottom was dry. His hands were untouched, no marks, no bruises. He didn't put up a fight against whoever did it to him."

"The wrong guy is dead. It was supposed to be the Governor, but something happened," Donnie said. "I found this in the Governor's cottage." Donnie produced a legal looking document. Opening it, I saw the words `Last Will & Testament'.

Who is the beneficiary?" Butch asked.

"Jason Bland."

"Bingo!" I said. "Did the Governor sign it?"

"Yes and no," Donnie said. "Look!" He opened the will to the last page. It was signed, Stonewall Jackson Johnson. "Joe said it was his signature, but not his name. He's William E. Johnson. He's a bit confused."

"It's been a good night's work. Why don't you guys go home and get some rest. Meet me back here at 6:00," Butch instructed the men. They got up to leave.

"I have a brand new cruiser and it will be a mud pie by the time I'm done with it," Donnie muttered.

"How did you get so dirty?" I asked.

"I slipped down an embankment, coming back from the Governor's house. I kept the evidence dry, at least.

"Donnie, I have a full service laundry here. Go take a shower and steam and I can get you cleaned up, pronto," I said. All the men were gone except for Butch and Donnie.

"I have to stay here for the day, but I might take you up on the shower," Butch said, taking a quick glance at Donnie. I knew what that glance meant.

Donnie was a member of the fraternity. He looked me over slowly. "Is Clydesdale that old friend of yours you told me about?" he asked.

"He sure as hell is," Butch answered.

"Give me your clothes and we can talk about old times later," I said. I gave them each a locker and took Donnie's mud caked uniform to the washer and dryer I had for towels. I was good at doing uniforms and knew just how to get the grungy mud out of them.

When I got back to the shower, both men were naked and looked good. Butch always had a Sean Connery look to him. Sean had aged, and so had Butch. His face had more character, his body had filled out, but regular exercise kept him firm. His body hair was downright shaggy and it contrasted attractively with his muscular body.

Donnie had a baby face and had been pudgy when he was younger. He was getting muscular. I bet Butch had something to do with that. He had a barrel chest, covered in long, silky, black hair. His cock was already half hard. I stripped and joined them. Donnie's eyes didn't exactly bug completely out of his head when he saw my cock, but they came close.

"Is this the guy you described as horse hung chimp?" Donnie asked.

"You got it. Clydesdale is the one," Butch said.

"It's bigger in real life than you described. What's it like hard."

"You'll know soon enough," I said. "Don't start anything you can't finish."

"Don't worry about Donnie. I've been training him. He's not finished with his training, but he's into it," Butch said. "He likes size."

As if to prove that, Donnie leaned over and licked my cock. As I'd guessed, one lick wasn't enough. I wasn't hard yet so he got a lot of my meat down his throat. He couldn't keep it in long. As I got harder, he had to give it up, but he sure was interested. Out of the corner of my eye I saw Donovan looking into the shower from the exercise area. He saw us and smiled.

"Butch, let's adjourn this party to the steam room where it's a bit more private," I said. We went into the steam room and I cranked up the heat. I was hard to do with Donnie attached to my cock, but I managed. I sat on the marble bench next to Butch and poor Donnie had the hard choice to make between the two cocks. He was a size queen, so mine had an allure, but Butch was well hung and handsome. Donnie was torn. He tried to suck both.

The problem was resolved when Donovan entered. It was pretty steamy by then and he couldn't see us clearly.

"Are you in here Clydesdale?" he asked, as if he didn't know. Donnie jumped, but I held his head to my cock.

"I sure am; just relaxing with my buddies," I answered. "I'm getting ready to have my balls drained, so don't come over unless you're thirsty and feel like helping our law enforcement officers relax." Donovan came up to us; he was already at half staff. Butch's cock was rock hard and standing straight up. Donovan was staring at it.

Butch stroked his cock, making a bead of precum emerge from his slit. "It tastes a lot better than it looks," Butch observed. Donovan hesitated. "Don't be shy, get to it!" Butch ordered. Donovan obeyed.

Butch was just as interested in Donovan as Donovan was in him. They were 69ing within a minute. Donovan was much more relaxed than he had been with Henry a few days earlier. Butch wasn't shy at all about sex and his relaxed attitude and enthusiasm spread to Donovan. There was nothing tentative about his enjoyment of man sex now.

You would think that two, very masculine men might have a hard time working out their roles in a sexual situation. They both went at it with no inhibitions or hang-ups. It was turbo charged sex. They were muscular, toned and well coordinated. They were also working each other into a pretty impressive state.

Donnie was doing a good job on me. I tried to reciprocate, but he would have none of that. He was a sucker. "Now Donnie, you've got to stop that or you're going to have a mouthful of cum," I told him. "That is, unless there's some other place you'd like for me to deposit my load." Donnie looked up to me and he almost cried. That boy wanted it bad.

"Butch, is this boy ready for the big leagues?" I asked. "I'm feeling like a trip down the tunnel of love," Butch looked up from nursing Donovan's cock.

"Don't worry, he knows the recreational potential of the ass," Butch said. He went back to Donovan's cock. "Oh baby!" he exclaimed as he encountered something tasty on Donovan's cock head. Donovan's dick must have reacted to the prospect of fucking.

"Open me up little, Daddy," Donnie whispered.

"Do you mind if we help this kid out?" Butch asked Donovan. They got up and walked over to Donnie's ass. Butch got Donnie off the floor then had him bend over. With a quick movement, he shoved his cock deep into Donnie's ass. Donnie jumped, and then sighed in pleasure. Butch fucked him vigorously for a few minutes. "Come over here," Butch said, motioning to Donovan the get closer. "Why don't you slip in and sample Donnie's love hole."

Donovan hung back. "I've never done this before," he murmured.

"There's a first time for everything!" Butch replied. Butch pulled out and guided Donovan over to Donnie. Butch got on his knees and sucked Donovan's cock to lubricate it, then guided it into Donnie's ass. He held Donovan's cock steady and made sure it hit the bull's eye.

Donovan couldn't have pumped more than six or seven times before he shot off, filling Donnie's ass with his spunk.

"He's ready for you Clydesdale," Butch said. "Get on the bench here, on your back Donnie. I want to see how you're doing." Butch got on the bench and cradled Donnie's head in his lap. "Do you take cock up the ass?" He asked Donovan.

Donovan said, "No, never done it. What about you?"

"Never use to, but now I take a trip on the wild side once and a while. Only for special occasions," Butch said. "Donnie, he loves it. It really rings his chimes. Clydesdale here is the acid test for a bottom. We'll see how Donnie does."

I was ready so I hoisted his legs on my shoulders and got my cock at Donnie's ass. I poked my cock head at the hole. It resisted some. I spit on my hand and lubricated my cock with the spit.

"I don't believe that fucker will fit!" Donovan said. He had gone soft after his orgasm and was still dripping. I pushed again and my cock head popped through the sphincter. Donnie moaned.

"I'm going to take it nice and slow, but I'm not going to stop until I'm all the way up your ass," I said. Donnie nodded. I pulled out again, and then poked it again. I was four or five inches in and decided, what the hell and I went deep.

"Holy shit!" Donnie cried.

"Damn!" Donovan muttered. He was hard again. He was close to me, so I reached out and stroked his cock.

"That's the fastest recovery I've ever seen," I said, stroking his cock a second time. "You're getting into this, aren't you?"

"Not really," Donovan said. He looked down saw his rock hard cock. It was oozing precum again. I must have looked a bit skeptical. He smiled and said, "Well, maybe you're right. I tell myself I'm not really into it, but I'm so fucking turned on."

Part 13

All good things must come to an end and while I was reflecting on Donovan's erection, my cock decided it had enough and it let loose. Stealth orgasms are pretty rare, but they're pretty impressive when they happen. I usually know when I'm on the edge, but I was completely off guard and I hooted and howled some as my seed flooded Donnie's ass.

Donnie popped too, so while I neatly filled his ass with man seed, he sprayed the entire steam room, coating Donovan and Butch in the process. His entire ass convulsed as he shot. I had to admit the contractions may have added five or six ejaculations to my orgasm. Orgasms are so short; I usually like the working up to the orgasm more than the event itself. For me the orgasm means the sex is over for a while and I feel a bit disappointed.

That wasn't the case with Donnie's orgasm; it was as enjoyable as it gets, entirely satisfactory for him and me. When I pulled out, my cock was still dribbling cum from my piss slit and my cock was coated with Donovan's load. He had dumped a big one in Donnie's hole.

"What a mess," Donovan said, as he looked at my dripping cock.

"Don't complain," I said, "Most of it's your cum!" He reached over and stroked my cock. I spurted some, so I caught my cock drool in my hand and spread it on Donovan's hard cock. Butch was watching and stroking his cock. Butch began shooting. He aimed directly at Donovan's meat, coating the cock with his cum. A volley of sperm hit my face. Donovan was having another orgasm. The next volley hit my chest and the third my navel.

"Fucking hot!" Butch said. "I like a guy who can shoot his scum three feet after he shot off a few minutes before. We need to do this again."

"Now?" Donnie asked. Donnie was both half hoping to keep it going, but was exhausted and wasted too. He needed a rest.

"Tonight maybe, we've got work to do today," Butch said. Our little play session ended and I cleaned up the steam room, while the other men dressed.

Butch and the rest of the policemen left the club around 10:30-11:00 and the morning man reopened the exercise room at noon. I went off to the Governor's cottage to see if there was any more information to be had there. Joe was there with CW. CW was sent to the cottage to handle the P.R. aspects of the story. The club wanted a staff member to handle newspaper and television reporters' questions.

CW was slick and convincing as he gave out false information about the situation. Old Governor's in ill health were common enough and the extent of the problem at the club was swept under the rug.

I asked Joe how the Governor had gotten out of the house and had time to sign a false will.

"I don't really know, I was watching the tube and before I knew it, it was three hours later and the Governor was gone," Joe said. "It's odd, because I don't normally take naps."

"What did you have for dinner?" I asked.

"Damn! That's it!" Joe exclaimed. "Dinner came from the main dining room, sent here by a friend, a guy named Donovan, one of the Governor's golfing partners. There must have been something in it."

"But the Governor didn't fall asleep?" CW said.

"There were separate meals, normal ones for Raleigh and me and a special one of easy to digest food for the Governor," Joe explained.

"CW, could you check with the dining room and see who ordered the dinner?" I asked. CW got Jefferson to check on it. He called, had a brief conversation and reported to us, there had been no dinner sent from the kitchen. The only odd thing was a $100.00 bill left to pay for some broken plates.

"That's odd," I said.

"It sure is. There's no cash here, everything is signed for and charged to the room or cottage," CW said. "No one would leave a $100.00 bill. Do you know this Donovan?"

"I do and my guess is it's a red herring, placed to confuse the investigation," I said. "Where are the plates from the dinner?"

"They were cleared away by the serving staff," Joe said. "I didn't recognize them; Raleigh didn't either. He commented on it."

"What did he say?"

"Just that they were new men," Joe said. "Barely men, in my estimation. Young and a bit officious. Like acting students trying to play servants. They weren't my type." Joe was a big man, he was wearing jeans and a flannel shirt, unbuttoned to show his hairy, barrel chest. The outline of his cock was clearly indicted in the wear marks on his jeans. CW and Joe seemed to have hit it off. CW was casting quick glances at Joe's bulge; Joe could see CW's trousers were slightly tented. I was pretty sure they had guessed the other's sexual preferences, but they weren't quite sure.

The phone rang. It was Raleigh. The Governor's daughter was going to let the Doctors at UVA give a progress report on the governor at 4:00. We were to put that message on the answering machine and give no further information out to the press. CW gave that information to the club's receptionist and to the guards at the gate. The guard called us back about ten minutes later and told us the television trucks immediate set off for Charlottesville. There was no more to do at the cottage.

Joe went to the kitchen and made us some sandwiches. He was a roast beef, cheddar and horseradish man. The sandwiches were a success. I had to be at the exercise area by 3:00 so I mentioned I had some time to kill. I had some thoughts about how to use the time. The sex that morning had been good, but like Chinese food, it left me wanting more. We were talking and the conversation turned to Joe's career as a High School coach.

"It must have been difficult when you were a black teacher in the high school," I said. "Lots of anxiety in the locker room I bet?"

Joe laughed. "When you look back at it, it's hard to believe it was as hard as it was," Joe said. "Just stupid little things were problems. People were afraid I would see their little darlings naked and even worse, they were afraid their boys would see me and discover the truth about black cocks."

"It was rough on the red neck kids. Athletics were real important to them, but some of them had a lot of baggage," Joe continued. "Most came around. Actually, most of their parents did too. Time and a winning season do wonders."

"You do have a real man's cock!" CW said. "Not that I noticed, of course!" We all laughed.

"I know, Raleigh told me you boys were all choirboys, innocent of the ways of the world," Joe said."You remind me of the boys I had on my teams in High School," Joe said to CW.

"You think I look like a football player?" CW asked incredulously.

"No, the tented pants!" Joe said, as he patted CW's rising cock. "Some of the white boys on the team were uneasy, but excited to have a black coach. I made it a point to never notice."

"Did they ever see you naked?" CW asked.

"A few times," Joe said. "Never went out of my way, but when it was natural, they had a chance to see me." He stood up and took his shirt off, and then he undid his belt and dropped his pants. He looked CW straight in the eye. "You aren't just a looker, are you?"

"Shit no!" CW exclaimed. He took all ten inches of Joe's cock into his mouth in a single swallow. He was like a snake eating his prey live. The black tube of flesh vanished into CW's throat.

"Damn, I didn't know he was a sword swallower," I said. I took my shirt off and dropped my pants. Joe watched me with interest.

"Raleigh said, you were a horse hung chimp and he sure got that right," Joe said. The way he said it was a compliment. "I haven't sucked up any red neck cum in years. Are you loaded?"

"I shot off earlier today, but it's been four hours, I should be recharged," I said.

Let's go in the bedroom and try a daisy chain," Joe said. CW didn't want to give up on Joe's cock for a second, but we got him into the bedroom and naked. Joe really wanted my cock and once he got it he was happy. CW returned to Joe's cock and I got to suck CW's drooling member. CW was revved up. When we switched positions, I found out, Joe was just as excited.

Joe's cock was a good inch and a half longer than mine, but mine was a good inch and a half thicker. I have a club; Joe had a probe. I felt a twitch in my ass. I worked a finger in the direction of Joe's ass and he didn't seem to mind at all.

When my finger reached Joe's hole he increased the flow of precum. His hole was already lubricated. Joe stopped sucking CW.

"Are you guys interested in kicking it up a notch?" Joe asked, "I'm just about as hot as you can get."

"Count me in!" CW said. "Versatile here."

"What about you?" Joe asked me.

"Top here, but to tell you the truth, there's an itching up my ass. I wouldn't mind having it scratched," I said.

Joe laughed. "I'm a top too, but have been thinking about some stretching exercises," he said. He looked at CW. "Open up, spread wide and sat ahhhhh!" He lifted CW's legs onto his shoulders, and then Joe's shoved his cock deep into CW's ass in a single movement. CW was caught off guard, but had no objection to the black cock in his ass. When he could talk again, he said, "Damn, that cock feels better than it tastes."

"I'm glad you like it," Joe said. "I usually don't ram a guy first thing, but there was nothing putting up any resistance." Joe was thrusting now, pulling almost all the way out and then going deep on each stroke.

It looks like you have some practice at that," I said.

"Not as much as I'd like," Joe said. "I haven't fucked anyone new in a year or so." He was watching CW reactions to the thrusts carefully. "You're okay?" he asked CW "It's a lot of meat." CW was whimpering. I think the deep strokes winded him a bit. Joe pulled out. "Let's rest a minute," he said.

"It would be a shame to waste that erection," I said. "I'd be willing to give it a try."

"To tell you the truth, I was kind of thinking about trying your cock, Clydesdale. I don't want to sound odd, but I'm curious. I've never taken a cock as thick as yours," Joe said. "Your cock turns me on."

"That sounds good to me," I said.

"I hate to ask this after I just screwed CW like a fucking pile driver, but can you take your time?" Joe asked. "I'm not that experienced as a bottom. I'm not sure I can take it. CW is a lot better at it than me."

"That's only because I like it so much," CW interjected. "You can pile drive me anytime you want, I'm willing! It was great."

"I'm a 65 year old man and I never liked the bottom much until a few years ago. Raleigh fucked me and he hit something special. "Joe continued."Something about your cock tells me it's special too."

"Are you ready?" I asked. Joe nodded.

"Do you have any poppers here?" CW asked. "They open you up some."

"There are some in Raleigh's room." Joe said. He got up and went to get them. When he returned, he got on his back on the edge of the bed.

"CW, do you feel like lubricating our friend's ass?" I asked. CW was more than enthusiastic. I lubricated my cock. Joe was watching, almost transfixed. I was excited anyway, but the cool slippery liquid felt wonderful and my cock responded accordingly.

"Damn, I don't believe that cock will fit into my ass," Joe said. "Is that precum oozing from your slit?"

"It sure is," I said. "100% pure red-neck cock jam. If you don't want to go ahead with this, just tell me, I'm okay with it anyway."

"My mind says no, but my cock says yes," Joe said. "I'm going with my cock. At least I'll give it the college try." I had my cock at his hole by now. I pushed. I didn't get far, but he wasn't clamped shut either. I stroked my cock and coaxed a big glob of precum from it. I wiped this over his hole and pushed again. CW was watching and opened the bottle of poppers and gave Joe a good snort. I watched Joe and when I saw the poppers take effect, I pushed again. This time my cock head popped into his ass. His ass ring was tight enough to peel back my foreskin, but I had lubricated the inside of the skin and my cock head too.

When I was three inches in I stopped. "Are you okay? I asked.

"Yes, but give me some time to adjust," Joe said. "Pop it through a few times and see if I loosen up." I pulled out and tried to push in again. He had tightened up. CW gave him another snort of poppers and he opened up. I made four of five quick thrusts through his sphincter and he was open.

"I'm going to give Clydesdale a sniff of the poppers," CW said. "Are you ready?" Joe nodded.

CW gave Joe an additional sniff, then I took a deep snort. The amyl went straight to my brain and cock. My cock glided deep into Joe's ass. His eyes glazed over while his ass clamped tightly, holding my cock. I tried to pull out, but Joe was holding my dick in place. It was as if a powerful vacuum had control of my cock.

I pulled out part way, but his ass sucked me back in. Joe had lost some of his erection as I popped through the sphincter. Now, he was rock hard and his precum was flowing again.

"Fucking hot!" CW exclaimed. He got on the bed, straddled Joe and sat back, impaling his ass on Joe's cock. Joe moaned. He also relaxed some, so I could pull out further and start pounding. I rammed him hard eight or nine times then pulled out because I was too close to shooting. As I pulled out, I saw Joe's pink rose bud and ass lining. It looked so delicate and fragile I pushed it back into the ass with my cock head. My cock is crude, vein covered and bloated. I was turned on.

I planned to just poke the rose bud into the hole, but my cock went deep. This time there was no trace of tenseness. My cock and his rectum had become friends. It was as if we were old fuck buddies who had been screwing for years.

CW began to moan. He shot off, and then got off of Joe's cock. CW had drained his balls and there was an array of big globs with ribbon-like tails of sperm covering his hairy chest. CW's man seed glistened white and shiny on Joe's dark skin. He must have had ten or twelve major ejaculations; it was an impressive display.

"Damn, I'm floating!" Joe said. "I'm high as a kite and it's your cock that's doing it."

"Cock intoxication?" I asked. He smiled and his eyes glazed over. His love tunnel was hot and steamy, molding itself to every contour of my cock. Joe was out of it, enjoying the cock and its relentless exploration of his ass. He came to. "Damn I want to shoot!" he exclaimed. "Have you ever had a black guy give your prostate a sperm bath?" he asked.

I looked into his eyes, pulled out of his ass and straddled him. Then I sat back and positioned his cock head at my hole. He shot off. I sat back further. He continued shooting as I let his cock slip deep into my ass. He was jerking and twitching at each ejaculation. When he was fully lodged, my cock exploded.

Part 14

I got a call from Butch that afternoon. He said, he would slip by in the evening and talk over the case with me. He wanted a briefing about the guests at the club. I told him I tended to have visitors in the evening after the exercise area closed.

Butch laughed. "You haven't lost your knack, have you?"

"It sure doesn't seem I've lost any on my allure," I said. "My cock isn't any smaller. I'm no dreamboat, but my cock still attracts attention."

"Your cock is bait. Guys take a nibble and then decide to deep throat it," Butch said. "Looking back, your fishing technique worked on me."

"It's my cock you liked?" I said, pretending to be surprised. "I thought it was my sparkling wit and rapier sharp intelligence."

Butch laughed again. "Your physical beauty did it!" he said. "That and your cock. I'll be by around 10:00. Leave the light on for me."

The afternoon was uneventful. Wilton and Temple were exercising, but seemed uneasy. They were trying to act normally, but Wilton seemed preoccupied. Temple was trying to put the make on an older man I hadn't seen before. Henry was also there and knew the man.

Henry said the man was Alastair Normund, a retired oilman from Texas. He was the chief financial support for the America for Christ Foundation. It was a "traditional values" type organization specializing in being anti-women and anti-gay. I could see Temple was making headway quickly. Alastair wasn't exactly drooling on the floor, but he was close.

Henry saw the same thing I did. He looked shocked. Temple was "helping" the older man with the exercise equipment, making sure there was a lot of physical contact. Normund was fat, flabby and had poor skin color, pale and pasty. He didn't attract young men often and the boyish good looks of Temple were all he could hope for in a man.

"I've known him for years," Henry whispered to me about Normund, "He's one of the Senator's chief financial backers. He's never shown any sign of being interested in me."

"You're too old, Henry," I said. "He likes chicken. All white meat I will bet."

"That must be it," murmured Henry.

"Don't worry, I still like you," I said. Henry almost doubled over in laughter.

"Thanks, I needed that!" he said, when he could finally talk again. Jefferson entered the room. When Alastair saw the black man, he turned even paler than normal. He looked disturbed. Temple saw an opportunity. He ushered Alastair into the shower room. A few minutes later I looked in the shower and they were gone; the stream room was running. Temple had moved fast.

Wilton stayed for a while and left. There were no more likely prospects in the club. After all of the excitement of the previous day, quiet was good. Temple and Alastair emerged from the steam room and went on their way.

The room was empty when Jefferson finished his exercise routine and came over to me to talk.

"Things are falling apart for our friends," he said. "I heard a conversation at lunch. They are planning to leave the country."

"Too much attention?"

"To many dead men," Jefferson said. "Wilton is worried about it; Temple doesn't give a shit. If I were Wilton, I'd make sure Temple wasn't walking behind me."

"You think it's that bad?"

"Yes I do," Jefferson said. "I was brought up in what they call an "underprivileged" part of Richmond. I knew some guys who didn't give a shit for a human life. They saw nothing wrong with killing a guy for his sneakers, if they were good sneakers, of course. Upper class white folk think paranoid madmen only live in the ghetto. It happens in good neighborhoods too."

"You think Temple is crazy?"

"He thinks he should have been the Prince of Wales and married Princess Di. The world owes him. He's never gotten what he deserves, but that's only because he deserves it all," Jefferson said. "The housekeeping staff says he breaks things in his room, smashes them to pieces. He screams at the maid."

"Thanks for the heads up," I said. "Is there any other gossip in the dining room? Does anyone know who I am?"

"You are the life saver in the exercise room," Jefferson said. "A few of the guys know you're hung, but none of the young men."

"Donovan is the guy who knows me?"

"That's him. He use to be a gay basher, but he's reformed," Jefferson said. "I put one and one together and figured he had a genital conversion."

"Genital connection, not conversion," I said. "The boy just found someone he liked." Jefferson went off to the showers. I went to the phone and called Butch. He needed to know about the plan to leave the country. Fifteen minutes later there were 60-75 police at the club with roadblocks on every possible way to leave and men with dogs patrolling the edge of the property.

The crime lab was parked in the side yard and the Club was locked down. Wilton was arrested with Temple and two other men. I found out there were simultaneous raids on offices in Richmond and Washington DC, as well as a beach house in Cape May and a house in Florida.

Once arrested, Wilton confessed to the investment fraud scheme and to killing Jason. Temple somehow escaped from the Club, but was found dead the next day. He fell off an embankment and broke his neck. In the papers, there was no mention of the blackmail scheme and no one officially connected Magnus' death with the scheme. There was nothing to indicate what had actually happened.

Butch ran a good organization and the Club's name did not appear in the papers either. My clients were happy with the outcome, but I wasn't sure exactly what had happened. I don't like loose ends and was vaguely dissatisfied. Two months later, I got a call from Donovan inviting me to a meeting at a remote hunting lodge on the Club's property. I was invited, as were Lonnie and Johnny, the kid who had explained how the scam worked.

The purpose of the get together was to tie up the loose ends. Since there had been no trial, there was no explanation of what had happened.

Donovan told me the party had another purpose, best described as being a farewell orgy. The arrests had put an end to the embezzlement scheme, but it had also ended a lot of good sex. He wanted to tie up some loose ends and at least say good-bye.

"The sex was a lot better than you had thought, wasn't it?" I said, when he told me this.

"It sure as shit was!" he replied. "To tell you the truth, the sex was good and a month later as I looked back, it seemed even better."

The lodge was on the backside of the club's property. It was the ultra secret retreat for those who needed to disappear for a week or two. The Lodge was a big, low, stone building built in the 1920s. It had its own kitchen, and was entirely secluded from the club. Donovan, Hal and Charley were the hosts. Butch was there with Donnie, his deputy, Raleigh, Jefferson, CW and my group. Henry was there too.

Fall had been damp and cool, but on the weekend of the meeting Indian summer broke out. The sky was a deep blue; the trees were brilliantly colored in red, orange and yellow. After a cool night the temperature rose to 80 degrees. It was nearly perfect. Hal greeted us at the lodge door in an improbably small Speedo swimsuit and told us to join them at the pool.

I hadn't brought trunks, but he said that wasn't a problem at all. The pool was on the side of the lodge and was covered in a glass green house. Everyone was there and either naked or nearly so. When we arrived, Butch began to tell the story of the arrest. Butch was good about giving credit where credit was due.

"Wilton told everything. Wilton confirmed all of Clydesdale's investigation. It started as a nice way to combine things Wilton liked, sex and money. At first it was the potential for sex and a real investment company. The problem for Wilton was the profit to him was only a few percentage points of the investment. He wanted a lot more money a lot faster."

"He also had a hot and heavy affair with one of his clients and discovered that sex with older millionaires can be very rewarding," Butch continued. "The whole plan turned into a scheme at this point. He quit his job when he realized, if the sex was good enough his clients didn't give a shit about the investments."

"One or two guys figured it out, but all were socially prominent and conservative politically. There was no way they could go to the police. Wilton was afraid his ass couldn't take the pounding it was getting from all of his clients, so he recruited several other men to join him, Jason and Temple being the first to join."

"I was the third," Johnny said. "At first, it seemed like a real opportunity, at least to me."

"The whole thing was plausible if you didn't look too deep," Donovan said. He looked at Johnnie like a starving cat at a bowl of tuna. Johnny was his type, thin, muscular and masculine. I glanced over at Henry and saw the same look.

"Anyway, there was a suicide that disturbed Wilton," Butch continued.

"Edward Jannet?" I asked.

"That's him. He was one of his earlier clients and Wilton pushed too far."

"I thought he was Temple's client," Johnny added. "I knew Wilton was pissed at Temple about an "incident". They never said exactly what it was, but I knew it involved an unexpected death. I had sort of thought it was a heart attack during sex."

"I thought Magus was Temple's client?" I asked/

"Jannet was Wilton's man. His death wasn't technically a murder. It was unintended collateral damage. His death wasn't part of the scheme," Butch said. "Wilton was in over his head. He loved the money and the sex, but he hadn't seen the whole scheme to the logical conclusion. The scheme continued along until there was a second death. That would be Clydesdale's friend, Magnus, I think."

"That was covered as an accident, but smelled to high heaven," I said.

"Wilton decided to move out of Richmond and ease his way into Washington. There's a lot more money and more conservative politicians in DC. This club was the way station."

"And the Governor was the main catch here at the club?" Raleigh asked.

"Yes. Jason hit the jackpot here when the Governor confused him with his son," Butch continued. "Jason was working the Governor on the side, hoping to get big bucks out of the man. Wilton didn't know the side plot. Wilton was worried by now. He had Temple here to keep a close eye on him. Johnny had vanished and Jason was being a bit strange."

"Jason made a big mistake; he told Temple his plans to get himself into the Governor's will. Temple told Wilton, hoping to get a percentage of the take. Wilton went ballistic. He knew a false will signed by an Alzheimer's patient didn't have a snowflakes chance in hell of being credible. The whole scheme would be exposed."

"Jason was implementing his plan by the time Wilton discovered it. He had drugged Raleigh and Joe already. Jason had the Governor at the pool and planned to drown him. The Governor didn't even resist, there were no bruises on his hands and arms. Wilton found them, hit Jason on the head and knocked him into the pool, then pulled the Governor out of the water. By the time he had the Governor safe Jason was dead. He drowned; it wasn't the blow that did it."

"You mean he didn't murder Jason?" Raleigh asked.

"No, it was manslaughter at worse, self defense otherwise. That's why we've been lenient on Wilton," Butch said. "He also confessed to everything and pleaded guilty. None of his clients' reputations would have survived a trial. Given that he was a cheat, scoundrel, whore and embezzler, he was a gentleman at the end."

"Who paid him off?" Donovan asked.

"I don't know and I'm not sure I want to know," Butch said.

"I think that's best," Raleigh added. "This is a pathetic affair with no one looking good."

"What got into Temple to escape? He could have easily gotten off with a good lawyer," I asked.

"I know the answer to that, I think" Johnny said. "Temple was a bit of a Southern Belle. He was beautiful in a boyish way, rather delicate and pretty. He was terrified of going to jail. He was convinced he would be gang raped by black guys and mutilated. He was a pure top; he said his ass was virgin. He said his ass had never been touched and never would be. I bet it was a night in the county lock up that scared him."

"He certainly liked to look at my meat but he got out of my way whenever I got close," Jefferson said.

"Shit, he should have talked to me. I know you're a bottom with a taste for white cock," CW said.

"Damn CW, I was hoping to have some secrets from this group," Jefferson said.

"Just think of it as free advertising," CW said, obviously not concerned. Most of the men laughed. The conversation continued as the details of the scheme were discussed. Hal served drinks and the party became more convivial.

Donovan ended up next to Henry and Johnny. Lonnie and Hal seemed to like Jefferson. Donnie liked that group too. Butch and Charley stayed near me and Raleigh. Everyone wanted sex, but no one wanted to shoot the starter's gun.

I took the bull by the horns. "Hey guys! We've just finished a long and difficult case and it ended about as well as it could have. It's time for celebration. I don't want you guys to think I'm a slut or something, but I'm the only one here who has seen you all naked and erect." There was a titter of laughter. "I know what you all like. I know that most of you can actually admit to yourself that you like it. How about celebrating with a no holes barred sex party? Let's let ourselves go and do what comes naturally." There was more laughter and some applause.

"Now, I hate to get technical, but when I say no holes barred you all know what hole I am talking about. You all know what I like to shove in that hole too. I may have more experience with this than the rest of you and this kind of party works if everyone is with the program. Does anyone have a problem with that?"

"Not me!" Donovan said. Everyone else murmured approval. Donovan made a dive for Johnny's cock. Henry looked disappointed, but the three of them worked things out pretty well it seemed to me.

Jefferson had tried to play down his attraction to white men, but he sure liked Donnie. He was looking at Butch from the corner of his eye too. I figured a southern, red neck policeman's dick in his ass would be just about perfect for Jefferson. The next time I looked, Donnie was slow fucking Jefferson. By then Raleigh was in Hal's ass and poor Hal was having the time of his life.

It's funny. I knew Hal well enough to know he didn't have any racial hang-ups, in the same way Jefferson had no problems with white people. There is a lot of racial baggage in the air though and sometimes sex can be enhanced by the suggestion of forbidden fruit. The middle-aged, Republican, businessman squirming on a black servant's cock and the Deputy's cock slipping deep into a black man's ass sure did the trick for all four men.

Johnny and Henry were 69ing. Donovan seemed to have a hard time figuring out where to fit into the sexual jigsaw. I wandered over and lubricated my cock. Henry and Johnny were in a tight ball and Johnny's ass was open, so I took advantage of the opportunity. Henry was shocked when he saw my cock gliding into Johnny's ass, just inches from his eyes, but he stayed put and enjoyed the show. Donovan saw the same thing. He lubricated his cock and eased it into Henry's rear end.

Henry jumped at the surprise attack, but when he saw it was Donovan, he smiled and adjusted his position so Donovan would have better access. For some reason, I thought Henry was being fucked for the first time and Henry wanted Donovan to be the one.

It wasn't a very neat afternoon. Cocks were dripping precum, asses were leaking cum, and there was sperm everywhere after the first hour of play. As the day turned into evening, everyone loosened up. Henry and Johnny both fucked Donovan. Much to my surprise, so did Jefferson. Donnie took Raleigh's cock twice. I was fucked by Charley and Hal. I fucked Butch for old time's sake.

All in all, it was a good party.

Part 15

There was one other bit of unfinished business. The next spring, I was invited to Hector's farm with John. As we drove there John filled me in on what had happened in Hector's relationship with Johnny. Hector and Johnny were still living together. The farm had been good for Johnny. At first he had been the caretaker, but he had a farming back ground as did Hector. They were developing it as a tree nursery and organic vegetable garden.

Johnnie had given up his quick rich schemes and was happy as a lark working the property. Hector's brother, Socrates, had died and left Hector enough money to get the thing under way.

"Do they have a strictly monogamous relationship now?" I asked.

"I'm not sure monogamous is the right world for it," John said. "They don't cheat on each other, but they do share. A threesome or foursome is fine as long as they share."

"Share and share alike is good for me."

We reached Hector's farm. The sign at the gate said Mt. Olympus Farm. Someone in the family had distinctly classical tastes. John called Hector from the gate and told him we were there. Hector asked us to close the gate behind us. We were the last of the guests expected that afternoon. We drove down a winding road through a wooded area and then crossed a broad pasture. The house looked quite small from a distance, but was larger close up. It was a beautiful sunny and clear afternoon.

There were several cars in the rear yard. Hector came out to greet us. He was wearing a towel.

"Is this a Toga party?" I asked.

"Not at all," Hector replied with a smile. "It's not that formal. Welcome to Mt. Olympus. My Grand Father was classical scholar. One son got half of the property, and called it Latium Farm. He named his sons after Roman Emperors. The other son, my father, got the other half and went Greek. For years I wished I was Homer rather than Hector. That was before the Simpsons!"

"We are at the Temple of Music in the side yard," Hector said. Johnny saw us and waved at from an opening in a tall boxwood hedge at the side of the house. He was nude and I realized what informal meant to Hector. We went through an opening the hedge and into a broad flower filled garden that focused on a screened in summer house. That was the Temple of Music. We were wearing shorts and tee shirts, and when Hector dropped his towel, we stripped.

Hector sprayed us with sun block lotion and we went to the Temple. The place was beautiful and lush in the way Virginia can be in a good spring. It seemed as if everything that could bloom was in bloom. The temple was a wooden pavilion made mostly of lattice and vines. The Temple of Music on Mt. Olympus farm sounded like it would be pretentious, but it was playful and informal. It was more of an architectural joke than an attempt at showing off.

We went in the Temple and found wicker chairs, a cooler filled with drinks and a table with food. The interior seemed dark compared to the bright sunlight. As my eyes adjusted I saw the most prominent feature of the room, a sling hanging from the ceiling. In the sling was none other than Senator Barton Smith. He had resigned his seat several months earlier. His wife had died of a particularly aggressive form of cancer and he decided to withdraw from public life.

John told me Senator Smith discovered life was too short to spend all of his remaining years in the closet. As I looked at him in the sling I saw his ass was wide open and glistening with lubricant and sperm. Standing next to him was Colin, Larry, John's next door neighbor. Raleigh and Joe were there too. Sperm was still dripping from Joe's cock so he must have been the last to fuck the former senator.

"I think you know most of the men here," Hector said. "This is just a fun afternoon in the country, but Barton offered to be part of the afternoon's entertainment." Hector stroked his cock to life and eased it into Barton's hole. "I guess you could say Barton had made peace with his sexual interests. I don't think he realized he was a bottom pig."

Hector was horse hung and Barton winched when knob popped through the sphincter. He sighed as the thick tube slid deep into his ass. The former Senator closed his eyes and relaxed as Hector thrust. "That's wonderful," Barton moaned.

Three men entered the Temple. It was Donovan and two men I didn't know. Donovan introduced them as Theo and Boomer.

Theo was a big bruiser of a man. He looked as if he was muscle bound, but he was agile. His tanned body showed signs of several scars and his nose had been broken many times. He looked like a street brawler. Boomer was a pale blond muscle stud. He too was huge.

I didn't know who Theo and Boomer were, or why they were here. I suddenly realized they probably were body guards or enforcers. I never found out exactly what Donovan did, but I guessed it had something to do with intelligence and was at a high level. I eventually figured out Donovan was an upper level fixer for conservative types. He cleaned up messes when they screwed up. I guessed Theo and Boomer did his dirty work when that was needed. They were the muscle when that was needed.

No one had a greater potential for making messes than Wilton and his gang. Apparently Theo and Boomer helped clear up too. Exactly what they did, I didn't know, but I suspected they may have been involved in Temple's "accident." They were at Hector's farm for other reasons however. As part of the Wilton cleanup project, they discovered Donovan had taken a trip on the wild side. When the three men compared notes they discovered they were all members of the club.

Apparently Theo and Boomer had spent years hiding their relationship from higher ups and were relieved when they discovered Donovan shared some of their tastes. They were even more relieved to find out Donovan shared all of their tastes. They liked the same sort of man. The trio liked masculine, well hung men. Donovan not only liked them, he had discovered a generous supply of them at the Culpepper Hunt Club.

Through Donovan's connection with Johnny he had met Hector. Theo and Boomer had been monogamous out of necessity. They wanted to sample some of Donovan's new found friends. They had visited Hector and Johnny in the winter and that had been a success. Donovan had also run into Senator Smith during the investigation and they had a hit it off. Smith had been playing with young men, but discovered he had been wasting his time you the young men. He liked being dominated by an aggressive man.

I later found out Donovan was the first to fuck Senator Smith. Donovan had also popped his cherry, and then had Theo and Boomer plug him. The Senator had been follower in the genteel school of gay sex. A quickie with a youngish looking boy had been the extent of his sexual experience. Having two gorillas like Theo and Boomer fuck him to the moon and back opened entirely new vistas of sexual satisfaction.

This afternoon spent in a sling was the next part of Donovan training scheme. He was converting Barton from a raised pinkie fag to a full service bottom pig. I'm not that good a judge of character. Donovan recognized something in Barton I hadn't guessed existed.

Just before we arrived Raleigh and Joe had alternated fucking the Senator for an hour. That had been a total success from the Senator's point of view. In the past he had only rarely even shaken the hand of a black man. For the last hour two impressive black cocks had probed his insides. Now Hector was working his magic. His slow but steady fucking approach reminded me of churning butter.

Barton was wearing out and needed a rest. Hector pulled out. Theo and Boomer helped the senator get out of the sling. I was shocked when Donovan took his place. When I met him he was a homophobic jerk. Now he was a bottom pig. He was a new man.

As soon as Donovan was ensconced in the sling Johnny came over and fucked him. Donovan loved that. Theo and Boomer came to me. Apparently I was on their dance cards. They had plans for me.

"That's a beauty," Theo said as he looked at my cock. "Donovan said it was a wonder."

"Did he give me a review?"

"He sure did," Boomer said. "Four stars for cock size, four stars for balls, four stars for attitude, and a minus one for beauty. Oh, I forgot. He gave you four stars plus for screwing technique."

I smiled. "Shit, I thought I'd get four stars for inward beauty?"

"Shit no!" Boomer exclaimed. "All your beauty is hanging out there for all to see! Do you want to play a little?" It wasn't a request. Theo was just being polite. He lifted me up until my cock was at his mouth level. He sniffed it, the licked it.

"It is a beauty!" he repeated. I'm small, but I do weigh 125 pounds. Theo held me aloft for five or six minutes without any visible effort. Fortunately I'm not offended by overly direct approaches, and I like size queens.

We didn't play a little. We played a lot. When you looked at Theo and Boomer you would guess they were tops. They loved the bottom and the larger the cock being forced in their ass, the more they liked it. Boomer and Theo weren't the delicate types. They wanted to feel big meat in their asses. Of course there were two asses and I had only one cock. Hector volunteered to help out. He possessed a horse cock too.

As a well educated and sophisticated college professor I wondered if Hector would like the rough and tumble sexual approach of Boomer and Theo. He had no problem at all. Hector was polite and courteous, but his cock, like mine, was so big it would have done Attila the Hun proud. No matter how careful and gentle Hector was his cock was a sphincter stretcher. That worked out well. Our two body guards liked it on the edge.

They were careful in selecting sexual partners, but everyone at Hector's party was acceptable. They wanted as much sex as they could manage. I got the impression they were little boys in a candy shop. They wanted it all. I sixty-nined Boomer as Hector did the same to Theo, and then we traded places. They were both physically big men, and I thought they were modestly endowed when I saw them first. That was an optical illusion. They were such big men the contrast between their massive bodies and their cocks made their organs look small. Boomer was uncut with double the foreskin he needed. His cock was still hidden even when fully erect.

I have an interest in foreskin exploration. In the few times I encountered the same situation, the precum trapped inside the skin was steamed, almost fermented. It was a strong and had a musky taste that was a turn on for me. Boomer liked to suck, and wanted to deep throat badly. He didn't get my entire cock down his throat but he got damn close.

Theo did swallow my entire cock. He wasn't much for precum, but his cock head was really sensitive and his organ twitched when I licked it the right way.

Hector had experience with the men on an earlier visit. He knew the men were lovers and in love with each other. He got them to sixty nine as we did some rectal massage with our cocks. This was a success. They went at it like dogs as we plowed their rears. As a couple there was no way they could suck and fuck at the same time. Our quartet was as good as it could be for them.

Donovan was being team fucked by the other men and had lost his normal reserve. Larry, my artist friend was handsome and friendly and his cock must have rung Donovan's chimes big time. A gang-bang-orgy combination sounds crude, but the reality was relaxed and friendly. It was a bit like a lab class in sex 101. The object was to see how much fun you could have and to discover new ways to have fun. As far as Theo and Boomer felt, our little experiment was the sexual equivalent of Einstein's Theory of Relativity.

Donovan had a very vocal orgasm and that set of a group climax. As far as I could tell we all shot off in the course of a minute. When it was over, Hector went to get sandwiches. We sat in the yard eating and talking.

I sat with former Senator Barton, Donovan, Johnny and Theo. Barton was a different man. He was more relaxed and personable. There had to be some reason he had been elected to office. You could sense some of his charm. His wife's death had shaken him. "I was positive if you did all the right things and said all the right words all would be well," he explained. "I was convinced if you played by the rules you could protect yourself from sin and be saved."

"My wife was a lovely woman without a mean bone in her body," he continued. "Some of my opponents said I got a double dose of meanness to average it out. I also got a double dose of pompousness too. I was a right-to-life man. I am opposed to narcotic pain killers. Shit, giving my druthers I'd bring back leaches and rely on faith healers. Nothing I wanted or would accept would contain her pain. You can believe anything you want, but you can't fool Mother Nature. Belief and reality aren't the same thing."

"You thought you will yourself to be straight?" I asked.

"That's probably the best way to put it," Barton said. "I wanted to be straight. I thought doing the right things and saying the right words might make it true."

"I'm afraid I fell into the same approach to my life." Donovan said. "I'm a big macho guy. There was no way I could be a fag,"

"We're making up for lost time now," Theo added. "I've had more fun in the last few months than I had in the previous 45 years.

After lunch we got together for a last fuck and suck session. Barton got back in the sling and took any and all customers. He wanted to take us all. He wanted us all to fuck him and for us all to shoot our seed in his ass. I had never been in a true gang bang before. I thought a gang bang would be mechanical and crude, but this was a nice, friendly gang bang. I was the last one to take a turn.

Sex can be messy, and Barton's hole was puffy and drooling man seed. I was three quarters hard and not too excited at the prospect of fucking him until my knob touched his hole. My cock head loved it. His ass lips all but kissed my knob as it poked in. His sphincter remained firm in spite of the hard use and he caressed my organ as it slipped in deep. As I filled him, sperm and other man juices oozed out of his hole.

I knew eight men had shot their load into his ass, two or three had several orgasms. Their seed lubricated the ass and coated my cock. It was smooth as silk, but still tight and Barton hadn't lost any of his desire. I always feel some excitement when I enter a guy's ass for the first time. Using my pals' cum as lubricant added a lot more to my excitement than I expected.

Somehow what I expected to be a quick poke turned into half hour of intense sexual connection. When I finally popped, Barton shot off too. He may have been new to the scene, but he was a total convert. When I met him first several months earlier he was a pompous, frightened jerk. He wasn't a Senator anymore, but at least he had a chance to be a human being.

About the Author

Bob Archman lives in rural Virginia in the shadow of the Blue Ridge and finds writing gay themed adventure fantasies and a pleasant way to spend time. He is interested in older, mature men many of whom aren't conventionally regarded as attractive. He discovered many years ago not even gay men can stay young forever. Most aren't flamboyant hairdressers, florists or interior decorators as is often portrayed in the media. Bob is interested in stories about everyday working guys who don't fit the stereotyped images of gay men.

Bob Archman is also the Author of *Clydedale & Company*. Available from Amazon.com, TheNazcaPlainsCorp.com or your local bookstore.

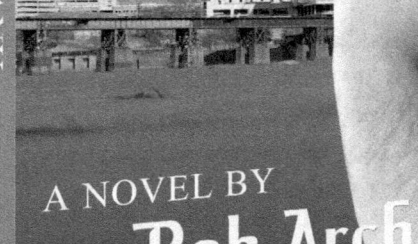

Archman

Clydesdale
& COMPANY

CLYDESDALE & COMPANY

A NOVEL BY
Bob Archman

A
BONER
BOOK